DIANE HARPWOOD was born in Halifax in 1945. She left school in 1962 and married in 1966. For two years she lived in the Far East with her husband, and on her return to England worked as a local authority Careers Officer until the birth of her daughter in 1973. The family moved to South Wales in 1974, and her son was born in 1976. A full-time housewife for many years, she has recently returned to work, as a clerical officer in the Department of Employment. She and her family now live in Yorkshire.

In 1980, Diane Harpwood was featured in the *Sunday Times* series 'A Life in the Day of'. Her article is one of the most remembered of the series: this book, her first, was commissioned on the strength of it. Writing it, she says, 'seemed like seducing Paul Newman – something I really wanted to do, but an overwhelming prospect.'

Sharp observation and biting wit characterise this brilliant fictional diary of a housewife. We meet our heroine ten years into marriage, negotiating the perils of daily domestic routine – the drama and boredom, frustrations and fulfilments of life as a wife and mother. Wittily, remorselessly, her diary records the truth behind the detergent ads: washing machines like bottomless pits, the malign magic of the sink that is never emptied, the refrigerator that never stays full, the never-ending meals – in short, the relentless daily round of the happy housewife. This is the black humour of everyday life as it is lived by millions. Hilarious and heartbreaking, it is the inside story of every girl's dream.

TEA & TRANQUILLISERS

BY DIANE HARPWOOD

The Diary of a Happy Housewife

Illustrations by Corinne Pearlman

Published by VIRAGO PRESS Limited 1981
41 William IV Street, London WC2N 4DB

Reprinted 1982, 1983, 1984

British Library Cataloguing in Publication Data

Harpwood, Diane
   Tea and tranquillisers.
   I. Title
   823′.914[F]   PR6058.A/

   ISBN 0-86068-124-6

Printed and bound in Great Britain
at Anchor Brendon Ltd, Tiptree, Essex

January

Monday 1st ☆ Started the New Year right, did the washing, had to, the laundry basket is not a bottomless pit. Don't know how I found the strength to tackle the washing after grappling with a two stone, very determined Katie who seems to have half a dozen legs and four or five arms. She'd rather spend all day in a stinking nappy than go through the ordeal of a wash.

Today I occupied myself in the gentle art of housekeeping, as on most days of most weeks of most years – making beds, my half of ours because David was still occupying his, and dusting furniture in case anybody called. Who's going to call? Who is there to call? Is there anybody out there? I couldn't hoover because it's broken and my dear one hasn't had the opportunity to repair it yet due to him being in bed till noon. 'Hi noon,' I said when he arose, poor pet he needs his rest, but a sling for his right arm would serve as well as the bed. Upstairs and down, downstairs and up I gaily trip in a valiant attempt to tidy our love nest. Like King Canute commanding the waves to cease their ebb and flow, I battle on with my endeavours to stem the torrent of untidiness which ever threatens to engulf us, but, alas, I have had to accept, as did he, that no amount of shouting can restrain the continuous inflow. Did he kill himself?

Thought I'd better get stuck into the ironing after lunch, had this sneaky little notion that David might

1

ask for a clean shirt to wear to work tomorrow. Katie doesn't like me to do the ironing; it's why she tried to grab the flex in the worn part where a clutch means instant death, and thought to trace it back to source at the wall socket. I put the ironing away after a little while, a very little while. Are all children as active as Katie? Lucy never was, or perhaps I was more able to cope first time round. It must be my fault. Doctors should research this phenomenon of infantile perpetual motion for the benefit of mankind – correction, womankind. Workers could put in their forty hours at one stretch and have the rest of the week off to help their harassed wives who don't qualify for the title.

After I'd prepared our evening meal, I cooked our evening meal and washed up after our evening meal. I didn't eat much of our evening meal because I was sick of the sight of it. I bathed the children and put them to bed and tidied the living room again. I sat down finally around eight, just in time to say cheerio to David who was going up the Crown for a darts match.

Tuesday 2nd ☆ This year is bound to bring a few changes, it'll bloody well have to. Lucy will be five in a fortnight, starting her second term at school. I'll be thirty in March, entering the slowed down zone, and David will be thirty-four in November, passed it – and a lot more besides. We'll have been married for ten years in February, and the second half of it spent here, miles from anywhere, especially home. Our first decade – we ought to make that a special occasion, if not for celebration then for mutual commiseration. Katie will be two in April, who knows, she may even be house-trained by the end of the year. The end of nappies, what more can I expect?

2

Friday 6th ✰ There's a man on our TV, a nice middle-aged man with a transatlantic accent and an understanding face: the kind of face middle-aged ladies might fancy. He says confidentially, just between him and me, smug smirk, that he knows more about bras than I do. 'Wouldn't be at all surprised chuck,' I said because I'm going through my Hilda Ogden period. On the other channel was a very together lady programme presenter who says it's time I started thinking about making chutney. 'All right chuck,' I promised, 'I'll give it some thought.' There wasn't anything on for the kids either.

Worked myself up to taking the decorations down today. Lucy and Katie helped. So it took ages. Bet the lights won't work next Christmas. Lucy wove them round the cardboard tube and God only knows what she did to the tube. It will probably be next Christmas before Energy Balls gets round to putting them away in the loft. He came home early, changed his clothes, and sat in front of the telly, chewing his thumb nail, lost to us.

Monday 9th ✰ Lucy started back to school today and was overjoyed to be there. Frantic hurtle round the house this am. even though I prepared everything last night.

Saw Les Girls at the school gates on this cold and frosty morning, catching up on everyone's news after the Christmas break. Lilian drove up in her mini Metro, expensive sheepskin, leather gloves and boots, just the right amount of make-up, short blonde hair loosely curled. She could bump into her husband's employer at any time and Hugh would immediately be marked down for promotion. I'd need twelve hours' notice to confront David's tea lady. Lilian asked me to go to the next meeting of the carnival committee. They have to decide how best to spend the funds left over from last year's village carnival. I said I'd go, of course, have hated myself all day as a result. I *always* give in to Lilian. I don't really know why I object to going; maybe because I don't want to be dragged out on a cold January night to be involved in an argument about the spare carnival funds, I couldn't care less about the spare carnival funds, but more likely because I hate the way I meekly fall in with everything Lilian says.

Pauline came back with me this morning. Neither of us could face housework, so while our youngest, her Scott and my Katie, fought it out on the hearthrug, we discussed the court case over a mug of tea. Kenny (her husband) was breathalysed last autumn. She's certain he'll lose his job along with his licence – he drives a delivery van for a local baker, and 'where will he get another one, kid, the way things are these days?'

I've been thinking about things today, my life, the bits I like and the bits I don't, and I've been thinking that I do all this thinking on my own, I never speak my thoughts to David, there never seems to be an opportunity. I think that's sad.

Wednesday 11th ☆ A Life in the Day of Jane Bennett. I start my day the Valium way at seven-twenty am., when my departing husband brings me a mug of tea and a Diazepan tablet. A Valium a day keeps psychiatrists at bay. At seven-twenty-one precisely my girls burst into the bedroom yelling and bawling. They've been up since six and are full of joie de vivre – can they be mine? I go a few rounds with Katie, she tries for my tea but I must have it. It's not fair, she should pick on someone her own size. When I've taken

4

ail I can, which isn't long, I drive them out of the bedroom screaming like a banshee and heaping curses on their beautiful innocent little heads like a hag from Macbeth. By half-past seven David is long gone and I've staggered into the bathroom for washing and dressing time. Lucy's OK, she can dress herself but Katie is another story. She and I go through a Rod Hull and Emu routine, except Katie has the Emu thoroughly licked when it comes to strength and determination. By eight o'clock, breakfast time, I'm exhausted, bad-tempered, drained of patience. It's the cumulative effect of a thousand identical mornings. Another day of soul-destroying solitude looms ahead. A dehumanising repetition of a detestable routine. I hurtle round the kitchen from frying pan to fridge and back again in response to the children's demands. I worry a lot about nutrition so they're used to having food shovelled down their throats: now, anything less than porridge, bacon and egg, tea and toast, and they're picketing outside the child welfare clinic.

Before half-past eight Lucy is glaring at me from the front door. She's always ready to go, hatted and coated and verging on panic about being late for school. We were once, and she's never forgotten nor forgiven me. While she glowers I frenziedly wipe Katie down with the dish cloth before the congealing porridge blocks up her nostrils and she suffocates to death.

We leave for school at twenty to nine, on time. Lucy visibly relaxes. It's a long cold walk to school and it usually rains.

Katie and me come back from school to face the overnight dirty dishes. I could cheerfully put a sledgehammer through the lot. Pauline once threw out a bucket full of dirty nappies because she simply couldn't face washing one more smelly diaper. Cathy's got an automatic washing machine.

On Fridays I go to the supermarket where I don't buy cigarettes, coffee, joints for Sundays, biscuits, cakes, sweets, frozen veg., washing-up liquid, tissues, kitchen paper, loo deodoriser, disinfectant, fabric conditioner, butter or squash. All these items are either too expensive or dispensable or both. Not smoking makes me constipated. Can that kill you too?

By ten o'clock the washing-up is done, dried and put away. The solid lumps of porridge have been scraped up (wonder if they'd do to bond the leaking crack in the washing machine?). I loathe, I hate, I abhor housework, nevertheless that's what I do next. Only trendy, middle-class lady journalists can get away with having mucky houses. Not that they want to; quite the reverse in fact. I've noticed that it's a compulsion with them to boast about how the cat was sick in the boeuf bourgignon. Or how they failed to notice that the stripped pine dresser – picked up in a junk shop for £15 – was feet thick in dust until friends wrote rude words on it with damp index fingers. Down here in Working-class Land you'd be excommunicated for far less than that. Among us lower orders cleanliness isn't next to godliness; they're one and the same thing.

At eleven I join Katie and we watch Playschool together. Katie has milk, I have tea and my mid-morning fantasy about another life. At 1 pm Katie and me have lunch. We share a simple meal of chips or packet soup and cups of tea. The hour after lunch is theoretically reserved for playing with Katie. In practice I usually have housework to do, but I try to fit in some chasing and racing and hiding and seeking.

We fetch Lucy from school at half-past three. She comes home with tall tales but true about what happened in school today. She's a fair mimic and so her story telling can be quite revealing as well as funny.

The kids and I eat at five, our main meal of the day. I

put David's in the oven to keep warm. Bathtime is at quarter to six, the girls adore it. I sit on the loo and watch them chuck water about.

David comes home around half-past six, tired out, to his two shining clean offspring, a sodden bathroom carpet and his evening meal.

I take the girls to bed at seven and read to them until they settle down to sleep.

Every day is exactly the same except I do miss seeing my friends at the school gates at weekends and David doesn't work on Sundays so there's no tea in bed. We're always broke, but wouldn't know we were poor if we didn't watch the holiday programmes on TV. They leave us gasping. Who goes on those foreign holidays at prices *from* £500 per person per week? Most of our married friends are in the same financial boat. We regard our monetary malaise as a temporary condition brought on by inflation, curable in time. If we didn't we'd go insane. We never go out, buy Chinese take-aways or fish and chips. We do take lots of walks, feed ducks, swing on swings and visit the library. I don't watch much TV but I read a lot and get my kicks from listening to Lennon and McCartney records.

Bedtime is usually around ten o'clock. Normally with a library book, occasionally with David if I'm lucky.

Sunday 15th ☆ Took Lucy and Katie to the playground as a reward for not waking up till seven o'clock and to avoid the holiday programmes on TV. 'Would you like to fly away?' Makes you sick.

Spaghetti bolognese for lunch, the ironing before it.

Monday 16th ☆ Lucy woke up covered in spots this

7

morning, chicken pox. I wish we had a telephone. David had to go to work to phone the doctor and then ask for half an hour off to come home and tell me what he's said. He confirmed my suspicions and said there is no treatment for chicken pox, I have to keep Lucy indoors until the spots have gone, about a fortnight he said, and keep her temperature down with junior aspirin. She's much better this evening after being violently sick this afternoon. I expect Katie will get it too. I'm confined to barracks again.

At least Lucy was able to celebrate her fifth birthday before the pox struck. The party went off very well. Cathy and Paul were the last parents to collect their offspring. They rolled up the garden path at six, stoned out of their minds but trying to hide it – no chance – full of bonhomie and duty-free whisky. Paul's just back from somewhere abroad, he's in the RAF, the booze is one of the compensations for having to go abroad for short spells all the time. I envied them, it seems such a good marriage. I can't imagine D and I getting happily, cosily drunk together on a Saturday afternoon, not if there was football on the telly.

Mrs Jenkins came back from her son's last week. She's been away over Christmas and New Year. She must get lonely and down too but she never shows it, she's always chirpy and busy, involved with the Over-Sixties club. Sometimes I think it's just a brave face. She must miss Geoff, her only son, now that he and his family have gone to live in London. Her husband died years ago but there is Ernest, her friend!

Friday 20th ☆ Five days of solitary. Five days confinement without adult company except for David who doesn't count because he's never home before half-past six and I'm in bed by ten. By the time he's eaten and I've washed-up and put the girls to bed I'm much too tired to make the effort of conversation and David wouldn't think of it. He needs his meals made, his clothes washed, not too much companionship, love and understanding in return. Perhaps he doesn't know I need them.

The doctor hasn't been – not even Avon called.

Sunday 22nd ☆ I doubt if love exists. It's just a word used to describe a violent emotion that bursts into fiery life in adolescence and dies quietly with maturity – like acne. It's mother nature's con-trick, necessary to ensure the survival of the species, the pairing and mating. But, once we're paired and mated, love is redundant. What then? Is there love after marriage? Love is just a euphemism for sex.

Tuesday 24th ☆ Afternoons are the worst. Lulled and dulled into a warm stupor by the heat from the fire. I sprawl on the floor with the girls and their toys and I know that it's wrong. The apathy and the stupor are wrong. I worry that they'll infect my children. Nothing penetrates my mind. I answer Katie, barely aware that I have. I watch TV with one eye and take no notice of what's on the screen and yet behind it all my mind is working. Like a wheel spinning without an axle, my mind whirrs on without direction or purpose or concrete thought. Oh, if only I could stop it.

Wednesday 25th ☆ Cathy's been, my depression's lifted, at least my depression vanished while she was here. I was lightened and brightened, it felt like heaven. I'm terrified that it will come back now that

Cathy has gone so I'm recording all this in my diary. It's a device to avoid returning to my tedious, boring, *depressing* afternoon chores. Thoughts of them loom like great black clouds.

Cathy came this morning, she stood under the porch, rain dripping from her fringe and plopping on to the pushchair. 'Well, I figured it this way, Jane,' she said, 'It was either come here for a natter and risk the baby getting chicken pox, or stay home on my own and put my head in the gas oven.' She came in. She's invited David and me to supper on Feb 4th – our wedding anniversary. She's going to ask Pauline and Kenny too, Kenny goes to court the Monday after.

We talked and talked, telling each other about our awful moods and disliking ourselves for our moodiness, trying to figure out why we are like it, but neither of us could come up with an answer. Theoretically we've both got everything we've ever wanted.

Cathy admitted to the same fault that I hate so much in myself, a tendency to go along with whatever people say when maybe I don't agree with their opinions. It's almost a reflex action. Cathy said that she'd tried to tackle it once, had made a vow to herself one night that from the following morning she'd say exactly what she thought. It so happened that the next morning she'd been talking to Janice, unfortunate because Janice is the sweetest nicest woman in the world. Janice had been rambling on about trousers for the kids, extolling the virtues of crimplene. Cathy had meant to keep her vow but hadn't wanted to hurt Janice's feelings. Eventually she blurted out, 'I don't like crimplene trousers.' She says she blushed scarlet and Janice's mouth fell open in shock. 'I felt such a fool,' she said today, 'What the hell do crimplene trousers matter! But, oh, you know how it is, Jane, the women at the school, they can go on for hours about household cleansers.'

I know what she means but it's not strictly fair. We're all sort of thrust together because our children happen to be of a similar age and in the same school. We all try to be friends but the only common ground in our narrowed down lives is housework or our kids.

Cathy confided her ambition to me too. She's having a stab at 'O' level History and begged me not to laugh. I didn't, I think it's wonderful. Now that Gareth and Lynsey are in school and Damian, the baby, is past the worst (he's ten months) she's decided to prepare herself for going back to work. 'I don't want to be a part-time canteen lady or something, Jane, I feel I could do more than that, not that I'm Einstein or anything.'

Her good looks apart, (Cathy's quite beautiful and revels in it), she's very shy and modest about herself. She told me about a girl she'd once met on a bus, the girl who'd really started her off on the education kick. 'We were coming back from Norwich on the bus one Saturday, can't remember why we weren't in the car. Anyway, it was packed, must have been twenty people standing in the aisle. It was a blistering hot day and I was very pregnant with Damian, I felt fat and unattractive and sweaty. Paul gave his seat to this girl and we started talking. She was gorgeous, really tanned, with a long curly perm and bare legs in scruffy sandals. She was wearing one of those Indian print skirts and a black T-shirt. She was really sexy, women with bare legs are sexy aren't they? I could see she fascinated Paul. Anyway, it turned out that she was a mature student at the university. She had a little boy and was divorced. She told us all about her life, I've never forgotten her and I've thought ever since that if she can do it with no husband to support her, then so can I.'

11

Cathy's doing a correspondence course, she can't get to the classes at the local college. She asked if I'd help her and I said I would, though I don't know how much help I'll be.

The rain had stopped by the time she left. I feel as if I hadn't known Cathy before today. I hope the baby hasn't caught the chicken pox. I don't know if it's infectious or contagious. My medical book isn't much use, it conflicts with what the doctor told David and says that 'dried scabs are not contagious.' Does that mean that wet ones are? Lucy's as fit as a fiddle, but she still has traces of the spots. I wonder if I could take them out for a walk or something now?

I've decided to continue with this record of my everyday life and my thoughts. It will be completely honest. I must face myself, warts and all. I don't know myself any more. I don't feel at ease just being 'me' any more and it bothers me. I've become unsure of myself.

Saturday 28th ☆ I left home tonight, flew the nest, scarpered. I'd had E-nough, and enough they say is as good as a feast, or in my case a glut. So the atmosphere in the old homestead has been a trifle chilled tonight.

I've been on my feet since half-past six this morning and my bum has scarcely come into contact with a chair all day. I've been making beds, tidying up, changing shitty nappies, tidying up, washing shitty nappies, tidying up, preparing, cooking and clearing up after breakfast, lunch and tea, washing the kitchen floor which is permanently filthy with bits of petrifying food and assorted muck carried in on everyone's shoes, except for today, when it was clean for a while. All of the aforementioned chores were carried out with the pack. The 'enfants terrible', they were today, 'et moi' have surged around the house in a scrimmage.

This evening I bathed the children, they soaked the new carpet which has lain in a string-bound roll since last September when we bought it. I brought them down to say goodnight to Daddy. I always do that to make sure they remember his name. I put them to bed, I tidied away the toys and went to make myself a drink which I intended to drink in solitude, in a chair that contained only me. He heard me, must have been the lid of the kettle, and he spoke to me. 'Are you making a cuppa, love?' he said. So blinded was I by rage, the shock of hearing his voice and the thwarting of my plans to make something solely and only for me for once that I picked a jar of jam from the pantry shelf instead of the jar of coffee, and I dropped it. It shattered, scattering splinters of lethal glass and smearing red jam all over my shining clean floor. It was the last straw, the bitter end, the death blow to my self-control and I let rip, shouting obscenities about him sitting on his fat backside blind, deaf and dumb to everything going on around him, and crying my eyes out. He said I'd only dropped a jar of jam for Chrissakes. That did it. I told him to piss off but, while he was still standing with his mouth open, I did. I flung on my coat and slammed out of the house in my slippers. They're probably ruined and he bought them for me for Christmas. I didn't know where to go, where was there to go? I slithered down the lane on the ice and crunchy snow and stomped up to the new estate where Cathy lives. God, it was cold but at least I was out of the house. I snuck past Lilian's, didn't want to have to explain why I was out in the snow in my slippers. I peeked in at the windows of the desirable architect-designed red brick residences – that architect must use a lot of carbon paper. Each and every one had its token woman in the kitchen, all there at their

13

sinks and worktops. I could see them through their double glazed, aluminium frames and brownly flowered roller blinds and they weren't complaining. I fancied that they all had a token pair of children sleeping upstairs underneath quilts from Marks and Spencer and a token husband taking his ease in their immaculate white-walled, brown and black with potted plant lounges and I felt rapped over the knuckles – and wet around the feet. I knocked at Cathy's but the babysitter told me they'd gone up to the Sergeant's Mess.

I slunk back home, chastened, perished and with my personality split. If you don't like it you shouldn't have joined. But the recruiting literature had me well and truly fooled. If you can't stand the heat get out of the kitchen. You mean there's an exit?

When I got home David was in the kitchen, feebly trying to clear up the jam and splintered glass. Beats me how men can captain industry, split the atom and remain complete failures at clearing up broken jam pots, reduced to quivering wrecks at the suggestion that they should change their own baby's nappy and/ or claim to be totally incapable of producing a palatable meal for their families once in a while. And to think that women are expected to melt tenderly at their boyish helplessness. I despise it.

'I don't know what the bloody hell's got into you lately,' he said.

'Do you know how long it is since I've been outside this door, David?' I said, tears in my eyes. 'Do you remember before Christmas when Lucy and Kate had whooping cough and I was busy wiping up vomit for six solid weeks. Have you noticed how every time you come home I'm here with the kids? Well, I haven't been anywhere in between.'

He put his arm round me, muttering consolingly,

and tried to stroke my hair but I shoved him away and he fell against the fridge and I stormed into the living room trembling and shouting that he knew nowt except how to repair combine harvesters. I felt a lot better for it, must do it again sometime. David said he didn't lead the life of Riley either, all work and bed with the odd pint thrown in to make life worth living, which is all true. He works hard and long and his work brings him problems and he has a crushing male hang-up about not earning enough to keep us all in luxury. But David chose his work, I was born into mine.

He made some coffee and brought me a fag and I snarled thank you. My hands shook so much that the cup rattled on the saucer. He says I should see the doctor. I said, 'And how am I supposed to phone for an appointment? There isn't a call box that works between here and Benton and anyway I can't get it all together enough to have the kids and myself ready at one and the same time and in time for the bus to the surgery. I can't do it. And what can the doctor do? Other women cope, it's me. And it's living here. What's so bloody marvellous about your job that we put half the country between us and home and family to get it?'

'Now don't start,' there was menace in his voice. He says I must stay in bed tomorrow morning, he'll see to the kids. Can't wait.

Sunday 29th ☆ Wish I knew somebody in the Lords Day Observance Society. There's just *got* to be a way of getting Sundays off. The kids were up before six, Lucy bouncing on the bed, Katie pushing her fingers into my eyes to try and force the lids open.

David allowed one puffy eye to appear over the edge

of the blanket and just a hint of jutting, unshaven chin.
'What the bloody hell's going on?' he croaked.

'They want their breakfast,' I said.

He pulled the bed-clothes back over his head. 'Clear
off,' he said. 'It's only quarter to six.'

'Go and have a biscuit,' I said faintly and with my
eyes closed. I was prone, exhausted and incapable of
movement. We shouldn't have stayed up to watch
Parkinson last night. I kicked him. 'You'd better get
up,' I muttered with my eyes still closed.

'Uh?... oh... yeah... in a minute.'

'Not in a minute. Now. They might be playing with the wall sockets or the carving knife.' I kicked him out of bed. He got up off the floor and pulled his dressing gown on, still asleep, hair sticking out in tufts, fourteen stone of sheer excitement and all mine.

I tottered downstairs at nine, they'd eaten half a pound of custard creams and most of a large packet of Rice Krispies. There was a great heap of them snap, crackle and swimming in a pint of milk on the kitchen floor. The floor that flowed with milk and money — cereals are expensive. It wasn't the children's fault but I had to shout at them because I couldn't see where David was, and Kate had filled her nappie, she stank, and her nappie was hanging down around her knees somewhere, saturated and dripping. I could see her cute round bum through the rubbers. Sunday bloody Sunday. Why did I stay in bed?

I used a mile and a half of Andrex on Katie's rear end, put her and Lucy in the bath and sat on the loo with a cup of coffee trying to come to terms with life.

Took the children for a walk this afternoon. Forced David to come with us. He walked ten yards ahead as if he'd forgotten we were there. I wasn't exactly purring at treading the same old paths on a biting January afternoon, but it was for Lucy and Kate. They jumped into the snowdrifts and slid on the ice. Katie thumped down, legs in the air, on her nappy-cushioned bottom, looked with awe at her own footprints in the snow. They asked a thousand questions about the snow and the berries and the cold and the early dark. It always falls on me to answer them, to chase them and to hide behind trees for them. How much easier and pleasanter all round it would be if David shared the load. We could all have come home and made tea together and eaten it round the fire and played 'I-spy'. Instead of that, he was in the living room, lounging on the settee with the papers, and the kids and I were in the kitchen toasting crumpets.

David's made his usual careful preparations for work tomorrow, laying out his clothes and winding up his alarm clocks, waste of time in this house. 'Where's my shirt? … Not that one … my blue striped with pockets …' He puts on his shirt, doing up most of the buttons, fastens his tie loosely round his neck and then pulls it all over his head carefully so that it stays right side out. It saves minutes in the mornings being able to shrug his shirt and tie on together and more or less fastened.

I think Lucy can go back to school tomorrow. She really wants to. Poor kid, she's been fed up to the teeth being kept in when she feels perfectly well.

Monday 30th ☆ Did the washing and cleaned the bedrooms, no success with the potty and it's such a fag taking pants off and putting nappies on and taking nappies off and putting pants on to go to school, the shop or wherever. Am tempted to give up and start again later.

Tuesday 31st ☆ Been to see the doc this evening; David made the appointment and nipped home in his lunch hour to tell me so. It was really great to see him, broke the day up, even though he couldn't stay long. He came home at half-past five this evening and took us all in the car. I feel quite cherished. Panicked about what to say to Dr Andrews so did as David suggested and described last Saturday night, the bolt for freedom, the tears etc. because I'd dropped a jar of jam. It must have sounded ridiculous. He seemed to know what was wrong immediately, didn't say much,

18

too busy, standing room only in the waiting room. He looked into my eyes, told me to hold my hands out in front of me, wrote a prescription, told me how and when to take the pills and he wants to see me again in a fortnight. I don't know what he's prescribed or why he prescribed it. I was too confused and embarrassed at wasting his time to interrogate him but I feel a bit better because he seemed sure he could help me. I meant to ask him all about chicken pox in case Katie gets it, but I didn't, of course. I've always got a pile of questions to ask, usually about the kids, but they never get asked. I always get the feeling that I'm keeping him from some life and death case with my silly trivia.

David says he'll nip into Benton tomorrow to pick up my prescription – there's just no end to this boy's talent.

Called at the supermarket on the way home, it was open late – had a night out really.

February

Wednesday 1st ☆ I've just had my two bed-time tablets and am now waiting for something to happen. The doctor's given me Valium. I'm a junkie. Wonder if I'll have psychedelic dreams.

Cathy's had Valium, she says they'll help my nerves. Cathy and Paul have invited D and I and Pauline and Kenny to supper on Saturday. It's to celebrate our anniversary and for Kenny to drown his sorrows before court on Monday. Pauline's cousin is getting married, she's terribly upset about it and I can't think why. The girl is twenty-four and the guy she's marrying is very nice etc., so Pauline says. So why the upset? I expect I'll find out on Saturday, we'll have time to talk.

Thursday 2nd ☆ Beginning to feel a lot better, long live Valium. I'm even eating food that I've cooked – there's a moral in that somewhere.

Lilian's off me, she went all frozen and tight-lipped at the school gates this afternoon. 'You're not taking Valium, Jane,' she said, shocked. Good God, it's but a step from here to heroin was the implication behind her disapproving movement of shoulders and chin.

'Aw pig off,' I wanted to say but couldn't due to lack of moral courage.

Cleaned through the house today – I *am* feeling

better – wish there was an evens chance it would stay that way.

Don't know what I can wear to Cathy's on Saturday. Haven't got anything that will make me feel attractive and alluring.

Saturday 4th ☆ Been to Cathy's party – have enjoyed it, it's done me good. We sat round the fire eating and talking after everyone else had gone. I do so enjoy talking.

Must go to bed now, the Great Lover wants to know if I'm writing a bloody book.

Monday 6th ☆ David woke me with my coffee at seven-nineteen, a minute early. Felt as if I had the sands of the Sahara in my eyes. Cathy thinks she may be pregnant again. She came to tell me today. She seemed more shaken at the idea than upset. She hasn't had a pregnancy test but, as she said, after three children it's hardly necessary. I tentatively mentioned not having it, unsure how she felt about that. She stared at the kitchen wall blankly, then looked at Damian playing on the rug. He's round and chubby and adorable. He turned to his mother and gave her a toothless grin. She looked at me, 'How could I?' she said, 'that's for other people, not me.' She says she isn't brave enough to face a future of would-have-beens, baby would have been one today etc. She's told Paul of her suspicions, and he was very supportive of whatever she decides. Cathy wishes he wouldn't leave it to her. She said 'If Paul told me not to have the baby, I wouldn't.'

Kenny got a year's ban from driving and a £100 fine. His mother has lent them the money to pay it.

Katie has the pox but isn't even remotely ill so I'm taking Lucy to school tomorrow, I think she's missed enough schooldays. I'll wrap Katie up well, keep her away from the other children and hope for the best.

I think I should have come on today too.

Wednesday 8th ☆ I'm pregnant. No, I'm not pregnant, I'm two days late and verging on the hysterical. I'll kill David. Should have stuck with the pill and the blinding headaches. Don't suppose I really did have a brain tumour.

Friday 10th ☆ Still no sign of my period and my fingernails are disappearing. Daren't take a Valium in case I'm pregnant, so I set off for school, looking as worn out and close to collapse as the push chair. No sympathy from Les Girls, they were too engrossed in Cathy's gossip.

I'm going to tell David to shove his cheque book where the monkeys shove their nuts, and demand real money. Actual cash in hand each week for housekeeping. I have the cheque book on Fridays to go to the supermarket and unnecessary instructions to 'take it easy' like he was allowing me into Robert Redford's bedroom equipped with a Janet Reger nightie. Then, shopping done, I have no apparent need for money during the week. Consequently, when I need cash to pay the fines on the library books, or for the bus fare to the library to pay the fines on the books, I have to ask him for it and I'm left feeling like an extortioner. So I shall request a reasonable amount and I shall manage it. Maybe man cannot live by bread alone but this woman would like to try. I could order myself a new dress from Pauline's mail order catalogue and pay for it in weekly instalments. I used to buy clothes from smart shops in big cities but not any more. I remember last year when David had to go into Norwich for something or other, he took Katie and me along for a ride. We parked in a back street just off the shopping centre, I sat there in the van, looking at the women walking back from the shops. They could have come from another planet. They wore make-up and carried bright plastic carrier bags with the names of fashion stores on them. I was shocked to realise that I didn't know what kind of clothes would be in those bags, hadn't an inkling of what colour or what style was the vogue, what style of shoes they would wear with them.

There's a part of me that says I'm being demanding and shrewish and that part feels guilty. I know we're hard up. It would be so clear cut if David were a tight-fisted pig, but he isn't, just unthinking and unaware. Is that always how it is?

Monday 13th ☆ Asked Lucy and Kate if they wouldn't mind getting lost for ten minutes while I drank my coffee. They did. It's the way I tell 'em.

On days like today when it's dark and pouring down and cold and Kate still has spots so I don't really want to take her out let alone walk all the way to school in a downpour and then all the way back again and the library books are overdue and I need bread and I can't draw the family allowance till tomorrow and I have one penny, two halfpennies and a button in my purse and I've forgotten to ask David for money because I was only semi-conscious when he left and I have a bit of a headache and I wish and wish and wish I had somewhere to go and Lilian is swinging the car keys from her leather gloved fingers and roars away from the school gates to spend the day with her mother-in-law in Norwich and all I have to come home to is the ironing and Terry Wogan I am, as I said to Kate, fed-up of this flamin' job.

Tuesday 14th ☆ St Valentine's Day, no card, no change, nobody loves me.

Wednesday 15th ☆ I'm not pregnant, had miscounted the days – sweet relief. I can't cope with another baby, couldn't take the lack of sleep.

Thursday 16th ☆ More snow. Have had to draw the family allowance. Pauline walked home from school with me this morning, she brought her catalogue with her and didn't think it shameful to draw out the family allowance. She thought I was brilliant to have lasted until Thursday.

Have had another close look of the catalogue tonight but I'm afraid to place an order. There's so much I'd like, pyjamas for Katie, slippers for Lucy, dressing gowns for them both, and a whole host of things for the house. What if I bought something and then couldn't manage to keep the payments up? Pauline said, exasperated 'You're only talking about fifty pence a week.' It's all right for her, she's working. She's got a job at El Dorado Bingo Club in Benton, she says it's great, like being paid to go out. She works evenings. Kenny's been sacked, he can't drive the delivery van and there's no other work at the bakery. Pauline says she has spells of blind panic when she thinks about the future, where and when will he get another job etc., but at the same time feels a whole lot brighter because of her own job. Broached the subject of housekeeping tonight. He didn't seem to be particularly interested in my carefully rehearsed statements about how having money in my purse would radically change my life. He did say it would mean he'd have to go to the bank every Friday in a tone of voice that suggested I'd asked him to climb the north face of the Eiger and leap the Suez canal. And he did say that to listen to me, he would have thought I had too much to do to contemplate gadding off to Benton whenever the fancy took me, but, as long as I wasn't asking for more money, only cash money, it was all right with him. He suggested fifteen pounds, I hung out for twenty and got it.

Saturday 18th ☆ Told Lucy and Kate that they could choose what we did today. They came dancing into the bedroom the second David had gone, flinging themselves on me, Katie wanting a cuddle. Was firm about my coffee today, wouldn't let her have any, my need was greater than hers. I have her to cope with, she only has me to contend with. Asked them what they'd like to do today. They were amazed; where was the screeching hag they've come to know and love?

'Grandma's,' said Lucy meaning my mother's and with a flicker of hope that maybe it was a bank holiday and we were about to surprise her with a week-end at Grandma's.

'Seaside,' said Kate.

'The sun *is* shining,' said Lucy trying for the jackpot, the question mark in her voice fading as she read my face, 'So can we go to the seaside?'

'Yes, we will.' I was determined; now I just had to convince David that it was a good idea.

They started shouting hurray and jigging about on

the bed and I told them to go and play somewhere else.

When David got home around noon we were all sitting in a row and hats and coats on the settee, waiting. My shopping bag, full of a picnic, was beside my feet, Lucy's toy hamper from Father Christmas lay beside hers and Katie hugged the buckets and spades.

David asked what was going on, I told him we were going to the beach. 'What?' he said – like a eunuch. 'There's snow on the ground.'

'Traces,' I said, 'mere traces.'

'We must be simple,' he remarked as we walked along the snow-edged path to the beach. Ours was the only car in the park.

'We'll have the beach to ourselves.' I said confidently.

In fact it was quite warm in the shelter of the rocks and the sun shone. It was heavenly to see both the children running around.

We'd only been back home maybe an hour when it came to be time to make the tea and bath the children and clear away the debris of the picnic, the polythene bag of dirty nappies and my trapped feeling came back again. What I really like to do on Saturdays is look round large stores and eat out in cafeterias. Those were the days.

Sunday 19th ☆ My children love me. More than that, they worship and adore me. What other conclusion can I draw? Take one step out of the kitchen and what happens? One infant voice or the other quavers tremulously, 'Mar-arm, where are you mar-arm?' And in the very instant that my bum touches the black bakelite ring – pow! they are there, Katie offering praise and encouragement. She's overcome with admiration: peeing into the toilet is an impossible feat for her. Lucy's quite happy to lean against the hand basin and watch. And as for leaving poor Mummy isolated in the kitchen to cook the Sunday lunch on her own, would they do that? They would not.

Houdini may have escaped his padlocks and chains but could he, I ask the world and challenge his successors, have evaded Lucy and Kate?

Monday 20th ☆ Awake around four, mug of coffee before the stallion went to work, gave it to Katie. Hadn't the strength to fight for my rights.

Took Lucy to school, came home, had a cuppa with Katie, did the washing, made the beds and tidied the house, fetched Lucy home from school, cooked tea, washed up, took the children to bed, read them a story, tidied the toys away, washed up after David's meal, sat down at eight, made supper at ten and now I've come to bed, ten-fifteen, with a book, high spot of my day.

Tuesday 21st ☆ Ditto except substitute ironing for washing and I forgot to include nappy-changing breaks.

Wednesday 22nd ☆ Lucy breaks up for half-term on Friday. My dad not so good again, has had to go for more check-ups at the hospital, his heart.

Lilian called in this morning, I was cleaning the bedrooms which gratified me: it's such a worthy thing to be caught doing. I could have been picking my nose. The vicar is selling those rustic plaques that you hang on the outside of houses to tell the world that you have a 'Bella Vista' or have finally 'Dunrovin'. She wanted to know if we wanted one and if so what do we want to name the house? I'm toying with 'Getoutofthisifyoucan'. I don't really want a rustic plaque, I don't like them much even supposing we could afford to buy one. Still, if the vicar really needs his organ replacing …

Thursday 23rd ☆ Cleaned the bedrooms, washed the nappies, cooked the meals, washed the dishes, tidied up, wouldn't be so bad if I liked it.
Motherhood is rather good
but I'd rather be a father.

Friday 24th ☆ Been to the supermarket, all out effort to make the twenty pounds housekeeping last this week, feel such a failure after all my grandiose words about managing.

Leighton called. 'This is Leighton your milkman,' he sang through the letter box. We pay at the end of each month which tends to confuse Leighton. 'Now,' he said flicking the flimsy pages of his thick accounts book apparently at random. 'You didn't have any milk the Tuesday of the week before last, and you had one extra yesterday,' he was looking puzzled, 'oh, and the fifth of this month you had two extra.' He was lost. 'Tell you what,' he said, 'Give me fourteen pounds twenty-eight pence.'

'All right,' I said because I could see he was having bother and I knew what was coming. I was sitting on the stairs by this time because it was all rather protracted.

'Now,' he said, more confident and with much brandishing of his pencil stub, which he licked. 'Fourteen pounds twenty-eight pence is what you

should pay if you hadn't cancelled on Tuesday of the week before last, and if you hadn't had one extra yesterday and if you hadn't had two extra on the fifth of the month. Right?'

'Right.'

'Right. So if I give you fifty-one,' he groped in his pocket, came out with a grubby handful of change, sorted through it and passed the required sum to me. 'Now, that's for the Tuesday of the week before last. Right. Now, you give me seventeen.' I did. 'That's for the one extra you had yesterday. Right?'

'Right.'

'Right. Now you give me thirty-four.' I did. 'That's for the fifth of the month. Right?'

'Right.'

'Right. Well I'll get off then, I'm racing my pigeons tomorrow.'

Saturday 25th ☆ Lilian has had to forgive me for not buying a rustic plaque. She's been muttering about people not supporting the church all week. She would have made a wonderful Redcoat at Butlins or Auschwitz. She has vays off making you haff a community spirit. Lilian is the epitome of the kind of woman who frightens me to death. I can pick them out on sight, they're all about the same age for a start, fortyish, usually their children are grown up although Lilian is the exception there, Edward-like-the-prince was a little surprise ten years ago, her other two are in their late teens. She's big, not fat, kind of wide and bony, a ship in full sail. She's blonde, her hair is a bit schoolgirlish, cut off midway between her ears and her shoulders, it waves a bit and looks the same, always. She has sharp features, a wonderful complexion and nice teeth. She's attractive, lovely deep blue eyes and always nicely made up but she's so sure of everything, I'm daunted by her. I can't imagine Lilian ever being confused or uncertain about anything. She's a good cook, her house is immaculate, she's always busy, village and church things, but never harassed, her whole life is even and calm. I'll bet she never has to drag a shirt out of the ironing basket at midnight because her husband needs it for the following day. I can't imagine her washing or ironing or doing anything that would fluster or dishevel her. She must do, I know, women all have to, it's just hard to imagine. She must be a wonderful wife.

She came today to ask if David will look over a van the girl guides are thinking of buying for their camping trips. I expect he will.

She says I should have a hobby. She's right. I would have enjoyed talking to her if only I didn't hate myself for always falling into line with what she says.

Sunday 26th ☆ David's been to look at the van. He's been at Lilian's all afternoon, stayed for tea. 'You didn't mind did you?' he asked. I said I didn't, I was becoming addicted to being alone with the children. Think he guessed I was being sarcastic, he's quick that way. He sighed as if in pain. He remarked on what a beautiful place they have, so clean. Lilian made him coffee, delicious, and the homemade cake was out of this world. He'd had a long and interesting chat with Hugh (Lilian's husband) about UFOs. Wonder if Hugh really does wear thermal underwear. David says what a nice couple they are and why don't I get more friendly with Lilian, I'm always grumbling about being lonely. He'll be inviting them to supper next. I suppose I could get more friendly with Lilian. Then again, I could ski down Everest with a carnation up my nose.

31

Tuesday 28th ☆ Kate woke up at four this morning. Got her back to sleep again, though, pulled her into our bed between us and she dropped off. Think it was the lack of oxygen.

Reduced the overdraft to seven pounds. I hate it, I really hate it. My heart plummets when David gets out the accounts book at the end of each month. It's always the same, deducting last month's overdraft from this month's salary before we start. Wouldn't mind if we were extravagant and could say we'd bought this or that or had been to this, that or the other place. We haven't properly recovered from Christmas, we shouldn't have gone home really, the price of petrol etc. David said we couldn't afford it, but I needed the break.

March

Wednesday 1st ☆ St David's Day – no comment.

Thursday 2nd ☆ Cathy and I really enjoy our Thursday nights' swotting. We can talk uninterruptedly because the kids are in bed and we can say what we like without infant radar tuned in to every word. Paul, if he's home, goes out on Thursdays and David always stays in to do his writing-up.

I spin out my walk up there and back too. There's still a nip in the air but there's that glorious light and smell that promises spring will come after all. It makes me feel happy. The weather has a big effect on my moods.

Pauline came tonight, it was her night off. She was admiring Cathy's house, she would love to own her own home but says Kenny won't hear of it, 'I don't want weighing down with a mortgage round my neck' he says. Pauline says Kenny is a ball and chain round her ankles, she feels he's a dead weight that is dragging her down. Cathy asked her why she'd married him, she's always complaining about him. Pauline looked serious, she looked at the ashtray and concentrated on pushing the ash into little piles with the tip of her cigarette. 'I used to be fat, you see,' she said as if confessing to a terrible crime. 'Oh, you know how it is. I was seventeen, I hadn't a boyfriend, I wasn't pretty, I

33

was fat, I was, it's true. Kenny played football for Blackthorne Bridge,' she snorted, 'that made him a star in my eyes. You know what you're like at that age. I thought I was somebody when I was with him, do you remember that song "I'm in with the in crowd"? Well, I thought I was. Anyway, to keep him I had to let him have his way and ... well ... I got pregnant, and we got married.' Then she looked at us uncertainly. The confession had obviously made her feel wary.

It was a new idea to me. I suppose I'm lucky in that D and I want the same things from life. I can't imagine marriage without that.

Pauline was very low, she let it all hang out, said she feels that her life is over at 24. Cathy tried to encourage her to think of training for a proper job, Cathy's answer to everything. She told her about training schemes for married women. But Pauline wasn't interested. 'We need the money from the Bingo Hall, Cath,' she said. 'There's my cousin's wedding, we'll have to buy a nice present and there's clothes. I haven't anything to wear and the kids need all new. After that there'll be something else, there always is and I don't know how long it'll be before Kenny gets another job.'

Cathy loaned Pauline a dress for the wedding, she'll have to shorten it about a foot but I haven't seen Pauline look as happy for ages as she did when she tried it on. I'm taking Lucy's best dress up tomorrow, it should fit Karen.

Pauline doesn't want to go to the wedding. We said she'd enjoy it, a meal she hadn't had to cook, no washing up etc. We spoke lightly but Pauline was serious. 'I'm very fond of this cousin,' she said. 'She's a lovely looking girl, well-educated, good job, goes abroad for holidays, her own car, the whole bit. This chap she's marrying is a labourer, a farm labourer, he has nothing and five years from now neither will she, except for a couple of kids, a pile of washing and nervous tension. I'm telling you now, I'll cry at her wedding.'

I think everything's just piling up on her, too much to do, no one to help her, lack of money, nothing, she feels, to look forward to. She says there *is* nothing to look forward to, she keeps going for the kids but they'll grow up and leave home and she worries about them living in the atmosphere at home. She says Kenny's like a lodger, they don't make love any more but she's not bothered it was all a big disappointment anyway and it's all right for me because David's a randy bugger. I've told him, he's thrilled to bits, promises to live up to it.

I feel tremendous sympathy for Pauline but totally incapable of helping – she says just talking helps, she has no one else to talk to.

Friday 3rd ☆ Supermarket tonight. Bought a stock of fags for David and me because they're cheaper there. Best part of three pounds to go up in smoke. I must try and stop again, feel I'm taking food out of my children's mouths. Have to face it, I am. Could have bought a joint with that money. They prefer sausage and chips. Is it more nourishing for them to eat piles of sausages and chips without argument or to have a roast beef dinner forced down their throats? Daren't ask the Health Visitor, she thinks we vote Conservative.

The sheets should be ready for ironing tomorrow unfortunately.

The pyjamas from the catalogue came today and I'm going to keep them even though we're broke. They're lovely. Lucy's dress fitted Karen well enough for her to wear it.

Saturday 4th ☆ Think of the nappy you first thought of, wash, it, then start again. Katie hasn't got a bladder, it's the Gulf Stream.

Sunday 5th ☆ Tried bribery and corruption with chocolate buttons – failed.

Tuesday 7th ☆ I've finished the ironing today. *I have finished the ironing today* – Chris Bonnington eat your heart out, it's not there. Mrs Jenkins called this afternoon, that's how I got through it, having someone to talk to while I dashed away with a rusty steam iron. She enjoyed her tea party with Ernest, her gentleman friend from the pensioner's club and was genuinely concerned that I might think her immoral. We had a cup of tea because Tony Blackburn said we should and she said the crocuses and snowdrops are looking lovely in the garden now. I told her of my momentous decision. I've decided to take up gardening for my hobby. It's cheap and I can do it without leaving the house – which were my criteria when looking for a hobby – and you never know, I might even get to like it.

Mrs J came to ask if I'd look after her animals while she's away. She said, 'I wouldn't ask, Jane, but there's nobody else.'

Wednesday 8th ☆ My father's a lot better, had a letter today, that's a weight off my mind.

Been to Mrs J's this afternoon to see about the animals. She has two geese, a cat, a dog and a budgie. I went round there with a chirpy, roll-my-sleeves-up-and-get-stuck-in kind of attitude. If I'd any wellies I'd have worn them. I clapped my hands together, rubbing them enthusiastically and said 'Right then, what's to be done?'

She deflated me instantly. 'Are you *sure* you can manage, Jane?'

'Course I can,' I said, put out, 'you're only going for two days.'

I know what it is, Mrs J is like all the rest. They think I'm clever but they rate my gumption and capability quotient as nil. They don't trust me when it comes to doing anything practical or requiring common sense. Cathy asks for my help with her 'O' level but she wouldn't let me within a yard of the scissors when she was cutting out her new curtains.

I don't care what they think, they're all wrong about me, I'm *looking forward* to looking after the animals. I wish I had a pair of dungarees and a hillbilly hat.

Mrs J was dubious about my gardening schemes too. I told her the thoughts I'd been having about landscaping, a sweeping rock garden with those enormous pale grey boulders, sloping down to the stream at the bottom of the garden, an arbour of sweetly scented roses, perhaps a small herb garden under the kitchen window where those rusting tools and broken bricks are now – that sort of thing. I'm really enthusiastic. Keeping livestock kind of fits in with my new image. Mrs J looked sceptical and said, 'Mmmm, well, here's a cutting off my spider plant to start you off.' She doesn't think I can do it.

Had an invitation to Lilian's saucepan party. Not going, don't believe in this party plan scheme, been conned too often in the past. Anyway we can't afford any saucepans.

Thursday 9th ☆ David's injured his foot, dropped a

heavy spanner on his big toe. It's not broken but the hospital have bandaged it up and it's very painful. He says he's going to work tomorrow but I don't see how he'll drive. I'm trying to convince him that he won't be able to drive, I want him here, I'm not quite as confident as I was about Mrs J's animals. That big gander's a swine.

Had a real cheek-flamer tonight, my most embarrassing moment. I've been to the saucepan soirée. I'm not a weak-minded conformist but if I'd missed out on the frying pans Lilian would have taken reprisal action. Cathy couldn't come because Paul's away, lucky devil.

We all sat about in Lilian's deep-down-clean lounge (she doesn't have a living room) wearing our best, pretending they were rags and feeling sorry for the demonstrator. She wasn't cut out for the party plan, smooth talk and sell technique. She was embarrassed and shy and stumbled over her Simmering Sheila saucepans in several sizes and Shirley-Sue non-stick skillets and she confused her Fiona Frying pans with her Olivia Omelette makers. Vive la différence. The star attraction was their Princess Pressure Cooker. It will cook anything under pressure, but then so will I.

Lilian's mother-in-law was there. She's one of those older women who always manage to look disapproving, as if they can smell something unpleasant all the time. When Lilian introduced us I thought her face was familiar but I couldn't place it. Of course when the penny dropped it was too late and Pauline had begun to tell them about the time we took the kids to see Father Christmas.

It was the Christmas before last, we'd so looked forward to the day out, we'd saved up the family allowance for weeks, wonderful self-control, but it was a disaster. For a start we had no warm clothes that would fit, we were both very heavy with child. It was seasonal. I remember Pauline's old trousers, she had to pin them to her vest – well, it was Kenny's vest. The kids were terrified of Father Christmas and wouldn't go near him. We ended up tottering to the benches in the square like exhausted pack mules and taking it in turns to look after the children and the bags. It was my turn to baby-sit when Lucy did her worst. I was sitting there shivering, with backache and stinging ice-caps where my nipples should have been, surrounded by three bursting plastic carriers, two pushchairs and three little girls, when Lucy said, 'I want to wee-wee.' My heart sank. There isn't a loo within five hundred yards of those benches and even if there had been, I couldn't have reached it in time. I stook up and looked round in wild panic to try and catch sight of Pauline and, in that second, Lucy had taken matters into her own hands. There she was, knickers round her ankles, down on her haunches, squatting right in front of the finest ever, twenty-feet tall, flown in from Sweden, Municipal Christmas Tree, a tell-tale scalding stream spilling onto the paving stones. 'Christ,' I thought, 'what if she fuses the lights.' Pauline's two, not wanting to miss the opportunity I suppose, crouched down on each side of Lucy and joined in the show.

Directly opposite us, with a panoramic view of the little scenario, was a bus queue at the head of which stood a middle-aged lady holding a tiny white poodle, one of those well-groomed ladies who return from an afternoon in town with a cake box tied up with blue ribbon dangling from one gloved hand and a bunch of freesias clasped in the other. She was also Lilian's mother-in-law. She looked in horror at Louise and Lucy and Karen and said loudly so that I would hear, 'Disgusting! They're like animals.' I was furious, really angry for once in my life, so I yelled back. 'It would be

OK if they were animals, wouldn't it? Like that poofy dog you're cuddling.' She was put out, I could see she was put out. Someone in the queue laughed as I remember and shouted 'Hear hear'. I was trembling. Lucy said, 'What's the matter, Mummy.' I said, 'Nothing, darling,' and pulled all their knickers up and hugged them and doled out sweets.

Pauline got a lot of the details wrong, thank God. And I don't think Poodle face remembered us. Maybe she didn't hear Pauline.

Friday 10th ☆ Mrs J has gone so I'm on my own, gawd help me. David didn't go to work today so he helped me shut the gander in. The dog took me for a walk. It's a labrador, big. The budgie isn't any bother.

David's promised to lay the bathroom carpet on Sunday. It's driving me mad. We bought it last September and it's been in the corner ever since.

We're to have another village carnival in June. Lilian says so.

Saturday 11th ☆ The gander went for me today, it turned on me with wings outspread and hissing. I screamed for help, Pauline and David were watching from our kitchen window, laughing. They came out, David limping, Pauline behind him saying 'shoo' quietly in case the gander got mad at her too and all the children crowding round. David drove it back into the hut with a stick. He says the goose must be laying, that's why the gander is so nasty. Mrs J could have warned me about this. I didn't find the cat till gone eleven tonight and the dog ran off over the field, devil of a job I had catching him. I'm going off gardening too, it needs so much expertise, all those technical

terms. What the devil is 'potting compost'? Sounds awful, I expect it smells.

Sunday 12th ☆ Decided to leave David before lunch today. I mean that. Before lunch today I decided that I would leave David at some time in the future when the children are old enough not to be affected by the split. I'm dying to tell him. I was seething, he made me furious, laying about in bed till past eleven then lolling around on the settee with a book till twelve by which time I'd fed and dressed the children, put the dinner on, washed the kitchen floor, washed mine and Lucy's hair, got steaming mad and finally accepted that there is no way he is going to change. All the things I did this morning aren't considered as work, they're just things that get done. His mother never complained so why should I? I'm not supposed to object to doing them, I'm supposed to subdue my spirit and rebellion at the unfairness of it all, subdue the bits that aren't already numbed by Valium, that is. I'm not even supposed to think it's unfair that I work and he rests. This week-end he is supposed to be laying the bathroom carpet. It's a wonder the children haven't got splinters in their feet. We've had it for six months. I was hoping he'd fill the holes in the dining room walls as well so that I could start decorating. We've had the paint longer than we've had the bathroom carpet.

If I tell him how I feel I'm accused of nagging and he looks innocent as if I was at fault and he was forgiving me.

I am a bad-tempered cow on Sundays and he did lay the carpet eventually, you can't see the joins. And if I did leave him, where would I go?

Monday 13th ☆ I'm not so sure that keeping this

diary is such a good idea after all. I'm uncovering so much anger and resentment. I feel trapped and I rail against my captivity and against the fact that there's never enough of anything from coffee to time off, and against the trivia that makes up my life. Oceans of anger and resentment will not change anything except me. I think maybe it's better left below the surface, admitting it serves no useful purpose. I don't want to be a crabbed bitter unhappy woman. It's important that I'm not. On me hangs the responsibility for building our family and that's a highly valued construction.

But cooking and cleaning things can't be important. No one pays them any attention except other women, and women in general aren't important, no one really gives what they do any attention, except other women, because all *they* do is cook and clean things. I find it very hard, impossible, to reconcile the way everyone says how important the family is with the rotten lack of attention paid to the housewife.

Wednesday *15th* ✩ Coming back from Benton market today I saw the women again, the women coming off shift from the sewing factory. I've seen them on the bus before and have always wondered whether I'd be like them ten years from now? They look so tired, their shopping bags look so heavy and they usually have to run for the bus on legs gnarled with varicose veins or encased in elastic stockings. They're mostly around my mother's age. Their skins look vaguely grimy, lined. Most of them seem happy, they've settled for their lives, many pass racy comments up and down the bus, teasing the young men workers. The older men workers travel by car. The women smile at Lucy and Kate and tell me that mine is the best time of life. Doesn't augur too well for the future.

Thursday 16th ☆ Bakers are on strike, want more dough. So do I, it gets harder to manage on my housekeeping money. Lilian doesn't approve of strikers, Pauline shrugs philosophically, I say 'up the workers' and worry about where I'll get bread and Cath didn't know there was a strike – too caught up in her 'O' level.

Friday 17th ☆ No bread at the supermarket. The newsreader on TV implied it was the fault of the housewives who panic buy. If I could afford it and had a freezer, I'd have panicked and have a stock of bread now. Christ, I can't even panic buy, there's just no way I can be a swinger. There must be some rich housewives about.

Cathy had the confirmation of her pregnancy today, the baby's due October. She seems settled to it now.

Saturday 18th ☆ I think I've been sexually assaulted. Took Lucy and Kate to Benton on the bus looking for bread. Told them it was a treasure hunt, and they had to keep their eyes open. Lucy spotted a queue outside a baker's shop (the family bakers aren't on strike) so we joined it. We stood and stood and the man behind me was a sexual pervert who kept pushing certain parts of his repulsive anatomy against me. I can't be absolutely certain what parts because I daren't turn round to look, that's why there is a shadow of doubt over whether or not I have been sexually assaulted. He

44

could, after all, have managed to get hold of a French loaf.

The children were fed-up to the teeth and showed it. I was terrified and becoming more and more upset, trying to keep myself between pervert and children and praying that Lucy wouldn't notice. I felt sick. It was strange, happening as it did amongst all those people, and yet no one knew and I hadn't the guts to speak out.

I told David about pervert when we got home, he was enraged, boiling; if he'd had the man here he would have strangled him. My hero.

Sunday 19th ✰ Went to Alcatraz with Lucy and Kate. David came too. We call the park Alcatraz because it's punitive to go there and no child has ever been known to escape the fifteen feet of wire mesh fence which surrounds it. Which is just as well because the council in all its wisdom chose to site it right beside the main road.

My birthday tomorrow. David should have remembered because I wrote it in the desk diary I bought him for Christmas. Against yesterday's date I wrote: 'Buy Jane a beautifully sentimental card and an astounding, amazing extravagant gift.' I'll probably get a loaf.

Monday 20th ✰ Lucy and Kate woke me by singing 'Happy Birthday, dear Mummy' at my bedside this morning – at six am. Made me feel small, they're wonderful kids, they deserve better than me.

Thirty now. Thirty is significant, like eighteen, only eighteen is good and thirty is bad. I thought David had forgotten, no card or mention of it when he left for work this morning. I smiled at him expectantly and said 'Thank you, darling' with a melting glance and love in my voice when he brought my coffee. Shook him rigid. After he'd gone I raced downstairs, hunting. I thought he must have hidden my card behind the corn flakes or somewhere, but no. I pulled the cushions off the settee, thinking it would be just like him to put it there amongst all the crumbs and debris that he knows I try to ignore. Nothing.

I spent half the morning slamming the washing machine around the kitchen in temper and cursing David to high heaven. As I said to Kate, I didn't mind about a present so much in view of the present economic climate, but I was upset about no card. Then, around eleven, must have been elevenish because Katie was watching the children's programme on TV, a van from the florist in Benton pulled up outside. Couldn't think they were coming here but there's only this house and Mrs J's, so I hoped, and they did come here. He'd sent me the most beautiful bunch of spring flowers. I was almost in tears. It wasn't because the card said, 'You thought I'd forgotten didn't you? You can stop swearing now. Happy birthday, David.' But because my father always used to buy me the first flowers of spring every year on my birthday and I thought David must have remembered. He hadn't as it turned out. It was just coincidence. He could have lied.

Receiving those flowers has made me feel feminine and that feels good. There's so little of that in my life nowadays, no pretty clothes, no perfume or fripperies, no money. It would be nice to *enjoy* being a woman again. When I go back to work. I can wait till then.

Stacks of cards from the families and Pauline and Lilian and Mrs J, a card and some perfumed talc from Cath. Feel a bit guilty about Mrs J, I'm sure I sent her home tight, she took her teeth out. She brought my card round and we finished off the sherry left from Christmas. She said, with a nostalgic boozy sigh looking at the pile of little clothes waiting to go out on the line, 'Oh, you know Jane, we always wanted more than one but Geoff was all we got.' She leaned over confidentially and whispered (because Katie was there) 'and we didn't stop trying till I was fifty.'

Tuesday 21st ☆ Glorious to see the sun and hear the birds and let Katie out. Wish she'd stay out, she comes back in every few minutes bringing half a ton of mud or assorted creepy crawlies with her.

David brought bread home from the little shop in Benton, two loaves! He said, 'You see, I do think of you.'

Wednesday 22nd ☆ Went to the library today, books were overdue and had to pay a fine. Had a look around the market, bought some fruit. They had some attractive clothes there, cheap too. Don't know if the clothes really were nice or if it's just that anything looks good to me now. Bought Mother's Day cards.

Thursday 23rd ☆ We can't afford to go home at Easter. Petrol is too expensive, David reckons it would take at least twenty pounds. I'm absolutely desolate. It's easy to see how families drift apart.

Friday 24th ☆ Angry words tonight. At least we spoke to each other. I'm sick to the teeth of him moping about the house and I said so. I've been keep-

47

ing it bottled up for so long, though, that I have a suspicion that it may have come out just a trifle tartly. He said what had he to be happy about and he was tired.

'*You're* tired! Christ, you should have to work one of my day and night shifts. All mine are doublers. You're never stuck in the house all the time, you're always going out.' I had lost my cool.

'I never go out.'

I gasped in disbelief at what I heard. 'I don't know how you have the effrontery to sit there and say that. You go to work every day bar Sunday and then you go out for a pint and playing darts.' I was very angry.

'Go to work! You're not calling that going out, are you? Christ, do you think I turn out at that ungodly hour six mornings out of seven just for the hell of it? And as for my pint on a week-end, I work hard enough for it.'

Subject closed. But it shouldn't have been. When poverty knocks at the door love flies out of the window as my mother always says. Inflation is doing for us.

Leighton came in the middle of all this. He thought it was the last Friday in the month.

Sunday 26th ☆ David played with his speedometer. I saw to the children, cooked the dinner, made the beds, washed up. Sat down to watch the film after lunch and he came in and turned over to watch the match. It's just one long ball game for men. The TV licence will be due next month, we'd forgotten about it. Hope they send us a reminder, don't want the girls talking about me like the lady on the TV ad. If she were a middle-class trendy they would all laugh and joke about it and court would have been an 'experience'. You have to be so respectable to be a member of the working class.

What do you do on Sundays if you're broke and have no relations near enough to visit?

Monday 27th ☆ Went to work on a Valium. David still brings one up with my morning coffee. Lucy and Kate forced an entry into the bedroom, I slyly swallowed most of my coffee in one gulp to make sure I got it, gave what was left to Katie. Watched her for signs of kidney rot but she seems to be all right. She flushes them out too often.

Tuesday 28th ☆ Cleaned downstairs. Watched Playschool with Katie, the presenter with the nice bum is back. I like a nice pair of buttocks on a man but most of all I like a fine pair of lusty thighs, they're what I'm watching when David is getting a kick out of soccer on TV. I'm a potential lecher, hope I don't grow up to be a dirty old woman, men are just sex objects to me. I am awful but I do like it.

Lucy brought paintings home, says she's making something really beautiful to bring home at Easter.

Wednesday 29th ☆ Must think about spring cleaning; the walls will have to be washed down, they're terrible, and God only knows what's on top of the wardrobe and the kitchen smells like a crematorium when I cook anything in the oven. I only wash the bits that show. Ought to wash the curtains too, try and get the nicotine stains out.

Thursday 30th ☆ Lucy's beautiful thing was an empty margarine tub covered in orange paper with

49

three egg sweets in it and a be-ribboned pipe cleaner handle on it. It's lovely, she must have worked hard on it. We've put it on the shelf with the best ornaments. She's broken up today. David got paid today, we are only two pounds overdrawn, thank God and the family allowance. That news did me more good than a holiday in the South of France without Kate.

Friday 31st ☆ Asleep by ten last night and didn't wake till twenty past seven this morning. Nine hours and twenty minutes. I'm getting phobic about sleep, know how Macbeth must have felt. Supermarket this afternoon – much pleasanter than going at night, shorter queues and I felt much more relaxed about what I bought as a result of last month's economic success. There's only four Fridays in April too, only four shopping weeks.

David's on holiday until Tuesday. We're taking Lucy and Kate out for the day on Monday. Looking forward to that.

This-is-Leighton-our-milkman called. I sat on the stairs and we went through the usual routine. He groped in his pocket to give me the thirty-four pence for the two pints I hadn't had a week ago last Wednesday, when a thought struck me. 'Leighton,' I said, 'shouldn't you be taking that money out of your bag instead of your pocket?' He wears a leather money bag around his neck. He stared at me for a moment, blank-faced, then the penny dropped and he looked terror-stricken. No wonder his books never balance.

April

Saturday 1st ☆ Glorious light in the sky, the song of the birds, the lambs in the fields, the new shoots and buds, the smell of the springtime.

Went to Norwich in the car, bought a new outfit for Katie, jumper and pleated skirt. She showed off, wanted to wear it to bed. She tried it on and turned this way and that. Poor little kid, she hardly knows what new clothes are. Bought a lovely dress for Lucy to wear on Katie's birthday too. Also bought a plasticine kit for Katie's birthday present, she'll love that. Lucy bought her a story book and we bought a jumper for James, my brother's son. Love spending money. We extravagantly had tea and cream cakes in a cafe too. Couldn't run to a meal. Bought chocolate eggs for Lucy and Katie. The price of them! And lots were buying the big expensive ones. How do they do it? Have attached long strings to ours while David was out tonight and have hidden them in the living room so that Lucy and Kate can have an egg hunt tomorrow.

Sunday 2nd ☆ David played with his tappits, think he adjusted them but isn't sure how it will affect his performance. Told him not to worry about it, I'm not Joan Collins.

I mentioned the garden, says he'll think about it. What could I say, I'm still thinking about spring cleaning. Suggested we go somewhere really jolly and vulgar and Easter-Monday-like tomorrow. A sea-side place where we can eat whelks and look at nasty souvenirs in shop windows and only smell the sea when the wind is blowing away from the fish and chip shops. If we're really lucky perhaps we'll get a jug of tea for the sands. Pity we can't go on a charabanc, like I did as a child.

Lucy and Kate were thrilled with the egg hunt, woke us at sixish to report on the funny strings all over the place.

Monday 3rd ☆ Went to Seacombe, it's awful, just what we wanted. David and I had a terrible souvenir contest. David won, with a faded, pale blue plastic lighthouse which doubles as an egg-timer. It's foul, flaking luminous yellow paint in the window spaces and trimmed with a posy of plastic anemones in luminous green and shocking pink and has 'A present from Seacombe' written across it in black letters. Lucy lost. She bought a plastic centipede which made my heart melt. She must have overheard us discussing the competition and decided to have a go, bless her. She was glad she'd lost because the loser had to keep the souvenirs and promise to put them on prominent display somewhere personal where he/she risked ridicule. We hadn't thought of Lucy being the loser. I bought sugar boobs with carmine nipples. Lucy put them on her dressing table between Paddington Bear and the Mr Men.

Had a picnic in the car and bought bags of chips. I hate cockles or whelks or whatever it was in my paper bag but the girls, surprisingly, loved them. When I was rich and single I used to think people like me, cheaply clothed and chip eating, were common.

Tuesday 4th ☆ It's snowing, had a shock when I looked through the window. I've been thinking about my uncertainty and I've come to the conclusion that it's because I feel inferior, I *am* inferior – and inadequate. I haven't always been so. These feelings have wormed their way into my mind and now they've taken over. There are no areas in which I feel confident any more. I don't know why that should be. Perhaps because I have no outside contact to sharpen me, no job to use me. Housework stifles me.

Before Lucy was born my ideas on raising children were so clear, I knew what I wanted to do and how I'd do it. I thought having children and bringing them up was *the* most important job. I suppose I still think that – but the things I thought important, being the person who guides them, the listener, the person who gets them interested in living, get pushed aside to make room for the housewife. I've always hated housework, always known that I did, and I didn't realise just how much of it there'd be. I see other women putting their housework first and time with their children second. I've made the same mistake. But has there been any choice? I give Katie paints and paper while I try to rush through the washing so that I'll have some time to paint with her. I take twenty minutes to set out the paper and mix the paints and find Katie's pinafore and brush. I go mad trying to keep one eye on the washing machine and one eye on Katie. After five minutes she's bored with painting and I'm left with the washing not done and a right bloody mess in the kitchen, so I'm the whole morning finishing the washing and clearing up the kitchen. That means bed-making and other jobs run into the afternoon when I could be taking Katie out. At quarter past three I'm usually dashing to school to collect Lucy. Another day wasted. Another day when I've failed to achieve anything. Mrs J says she always did her housework at night when Geoff was small. I've tried to do that but I like to relax in the evenings, sprawl in front of the telly with a book. I treasure those two hours between the girls' bedtime and mine because they're peaceful, no one wants me to do anything: and David objects to me washing at night, he says it's too noisy.

I'm not sure where all this leads me but I do know that I want to be successful as a mother and I don't think I am.

Maybe Pauline and Cathy are right when they say I think too much about it.

Wednesday 5th ☆ I'm really going to get stuck into training Katie tomorrow. She just sits Buddha-like on her pot at the moment, smiling pleasantly. I turn on taps, I read the Mr Men to her with terrifying drama but it's no good. I'd intended taking her and Lucy to Benton market today to buy her some pretty knickers as an inducement but it was too cold and still snowing. I've found some of Lucy's old ones to be going on with.

Made Katie's birthday cake today, lathered it in white butter icing and made a fairy out of a small doll. Looks quite nice, if sickly.

Thursday 6th ☆ Katie enjoyed her tea party. Mrs J came and brought her a doll. She'd crocheted clothes for it too. Katie was tickled pink.

I've missed Mother's Day, never had a card or breakfast in bed or anything. I'm hurt.

Saturday 8th ☆ Trying really hard with Katie's potty training, no success but lots of wee-wee. Ran out of clean pants by lunchtime so she's been naked round the rear all afternoon.

Ripped the dirty sheets off the beds, sang 'The Stripper' as I did it, made me feel racy. When I remade the beds I threw the clean sheets over the bed with a flourish, covering Lucy and Kate who were standing on the other side. They thought it was wonderful.

Tuesday 11th ☆ Rushed through the chores this morning and took Lucy and Kate for a walk to the stream this afternoon. Kate loves to throw stones into it. Had to put her back into a nappy to go, they don't make bags big enough to hold the necessary number of spare pants. Every time I look at her her pants are wet.

Asked David if he'd talk to me tonight. I was desperate. The children never stop talking, I exaggerate not, but it hardly merits the title of conversation. Katie says, 'What's that?', knowing perfectly well what that is. 'An apple,' I reply. She only says things like that to shame me and make everyone in earshot think she's never had one.

'Why?' She goes on.

'Because it's the fruit of an apple tree.' I try to live up to the expectations of the child expert in the magazine.

'Why?'

'It just is, that's all.'

'Why?'

It wasn't a lot better with David, we're not used to conversing. When we're in company, which isn't often but it does occasionally happen, I'm often astounded to hear him express views I didn't know he held. He knows even less about me.

Thursday 13th ☆ Health Visitor came today, Katie's annual development check. She's normal for her age. Comforting. I told her how little sleep she has, she said not to worry, she'll take what she needs. I dared to say that I was getting very tired. She shrugged. How can I be a good mother *and* go without enough sleep? Wasn't it the Gestapo who used to deprive people of sleep as an effective torture? MI5 should recruit mothers of infants for espionage duties.

The house was a tip, she won't come if it's tidy. I was flopping around in my dressing gown until gone ten, seems pointless to get dressed, and there were toys everywhere. Haven't hoovered since Tuesday so the carpet was full of bits. Thank God she didn't go upstairs. She said Katie was big for her age. I said, with an ingratiating giggle, that she was heavy and I had difficulty lifting and carrying her now. I wonder if there is a rule of proportion governing the size and weight of children and their mothers, like fish and tanks. I've heard that fish will only grow to the size their tank will allow. Comforting.

We were talking about our families at Cathy's tonight. Pauline came. I said I wished I lived nearer to mine, Pauline wishes she lived miles away from hers. She'd been arguing with her mother again. Pauline has a teenage sister who's becoming a bit wild, promiscuous. Pauline wants her to go on the pill, Pauline's mother is horrified at the idea. I said I'd probably get the same reaction from my mother if I had a teenage sister. Cathy said her mother would have turned the girl's mind so against sex with her stories that the problem would never arise.

'She used to go on to me, I'm the eldest you see, about how my father would come home drunk and insist on having his oats. It amounted to rape the way my mum told it. I understand how she must have felt now, but there was a time when I hated her for talking to me like it. I blamed her for giving me complexes. But Paul's helped a lot.'

Pauline said her mother had never talked to her at all, just hinted that there were 'things' she shouldn't do. 'I don't remember talking to my parents much about anything. If I tried, my mother always used to stop me dead by saying 'our Pauline's like …' I was always like somebody else, a relative, I was never me. It put me off talking to her. I wanted to shout 'I'm not like anybody else, I'm me.' She hasn't been the same since Scott was born, I have a son now you see, she never had a boy. She can't bring herself to like my Scott, she doesn't treat him the same as the girls.'

I was shocked. Imagine a grandmother favouring some of her grandchildren over others. Mothers and sons, there's something in that old saying, my mother has a thing about my brother, she's positively servile towards him. Pauline said the favouritism used to hurt her but she's used to it now, 'I shouldn't let her upset me, she doesn't know she's doing it. It's little things, like not so long since, when we all went for tea. They had to go out somewhere before tea, she left me to cook the chips and set the table and all that. Now if it'd been our Marilyn [Pauline's oldest sister] and her husband and the kids, she wouldn't have gone out for a start. She'd have been there all spruced up with her pinny on, like you'd expect if she was looking forward to seeing you. And she wouldn't make chips for our Marilyn, she bakes and makes jelly for her kids. I know it sounds nothing, I shouldn't let it get to me. Kenny can see no wrong in her and she thinks he's Mr Wonderful.'

Sunday 16th ✩ Katie ate Lucy's sugar boobs this morning. I can stop worrying about her growing into a sexual deviant now.

Told David to clear off into the garden and potter. It's like having a piece of grit in my eyes, watching him sit about. He did make me laugh though. Images of

David – sitting in the armchair in his boilersuit, frowning over the gardening book, thoroughly bewildered and puzzled. 'What's a perennial? Aren't narcissi daffodils? Well, what's an annual then?'

Next seen from the kitchen window, he was crossing the garden but now he was sporting his denim cap too. What every man of the soil should wear. He was holding a rake, a fork and a spade in one hand and looked baffled. He looked up and saw me and said, completely serious, 'I think I'll have a cup of coffee now.'

'But you haven't started yet,' I said.

'I need to think,' he said rubbing his nose with the back of his hand. 'I'll have to work this out.' He hadn't a clue where to start.

Monday 17th ☆ Lucy back to school today, not looking forward to it so much this time. She's enjoyed playing out with Katie. I'm back in contact with the world through the girls at the school gates. Janice was beaming today, they're going to apply for a grant to have a bathroom put in. Janice shames me, she's so sweet and modest with her ambitions. Imagine being delighted over the prospect of a bathroom. I don't know how she's managed, she has four children.

Lilian says she'll pop up to see me some time. I'll have to keep the house clean every day until she's been. Lil and Hugh are going to Spain for their holidays and I thought they were posh. Cathy didn't look so well this morning, better this afternoon. It's the baby and his teeth or rather his lack of them, and the effects of pregnancy I suppose. Paul is away on a long trip, three or four months. She isn't sleeping. They never tell you at these ante-natal clinics that a requirement for motherhood is going without enough sleep for maybe years. I was left with the distinct impression that after the first six weeks or so, if the baby was comfortable, warm and fed, she would sleep the night away. They should tell the babies.

Pauline walked back with me for a cuppa, Katie and Scott played at World War II with toys for weapons. She's not speaking to Kenny but she doesn't think he's noticed. Told her David had seen them in the Crown on Saturday night. It was as if I'd shouted 'vasectomy' in Mothercare. 'Don't mention it, kid, just don.'t mention it.' She'd made him take her out with him and if you'd seen the face on him you'd have thought she'd asked him for a fiver or something. He's banned her from going out with the girls from work after the last time – the hen party from which she came home drunk at two in the morning. So she said if that was the case he could bloody well take her and they'd both suffer. 'He was as mad as hell, had to sit with me, couldn't prop up the bar and play at men with all the other little boys.'

I asked her how she'd managed to train Scott. She didn't seem to know, just put him in pants and kept trying him on the pot until one day the penny dropped.

Tuesday 18th ☆ Bumped into Mrs J in the shop. She was drawn up beside the frail stand of tights, looked like a juggernaut parked at a petrol pump. ' 'Ere,' she said brandishing a packet of outsize and beckoning me over, 'do you think these will do for me?'

I was in tucks but daren't show even a hint of a smile. I expressed my doubts because of her arthritic hip, advised her to stick to stockings. 'Don't sell 'em 'ere, love.'

So I took the tights to the counter and paid for them

with my shopping, she was too embarrassed, afraid Peggy and co. in the shop would laugh. She's going Old Tyme dancing at the pensioner's club with Ernest, her gentleman. She's seeing a lot of Ernest, never in nowadays.

Wednesday 19th ☆ I haven't laughed so much in a long time. Mrs J has been – with her tights on. She walked in with her legs apart and stiff, like a combination of a toddler with a soaking nappy and a robot. To negotiate the step, she had to turn slowly sideways, swinging her right leg in a wide curve. She lifted her skirt to show me she'd only been able to hoist them to knee level. 'I'd never get on a bus,' she said, 'and I don't know what I'm laughing at, they were fifty bleedin' pence.'

Saturday 22nd ☆ Why do I cling to the naïve notion that Saturdays are different?

Suggested to David that we find another hobby, gardening's out. 'Oh, yeah,' he said, his eyes still on the TV. 'Well, they've asked me to join the darts team but I thought you'd object.'

It's the innocence that kills me. He must have known what I meant, a hobby to share. I've decided to read his library books, at least we'll have something to talk about though I don't know if I'll enjoy sci-fi and westerns any more than he'd enjoy my books about people. I ordered some new, recently published, books from the library, always read the reviews in the Sunday paper, fantasise about one day actually buying the books to keep forever, and then order them from the library. My latest selection is very good, staggering to read about realistic women characters who have

61

thoughts not unlike my own. Staggering and enjoyable, even if they are usually married to lecturers and similar posh professional types. Like a bit of glamour in my books.

Sunday 23rd ☆ Took Lucy and Kate for a walk along the path behind the swings as a change from a walk along the path in front of the swings. David was walking ahead and didn't know which way to go when he came to the part where the pathway forks. Didn't know whether to fork off to the left or fork off to the right or fork off home. Lucy said 'Mummy knows.' For some reason her remark made me realise just how little David knows of our life, of what we get up to when he's not around, which is most of the time. I asked him tonight if he ever wonders if I'm bringing the children up properly. Does he ever worry that I may be one of those who sit their children in front of the TV, the sinners, for amusement? If I were him I would. He said he never gave it a thought, the kids seemed all right to him. I don't know whether to be flattered by his confidence or annoyed at his lack of interest and complete ignorance of the importance of a mother's role. It is important, isn't it?

Tuesday 25th ☆ If an American sex symbol – male – ever orders me – in honeyed reassuring transatlantic tones – to beam down to the surface of an alien planet, I shall have no qualms about it, not a vestige of fear or uncertainty, I *know* how to go about dispersing and transferring my molecules and so does my grandad and he's 85 and was born under gaslight. All this we've learnt from television. God Bless the BBC.

I've been reading David's science fiction library

books. I've found them all terribly disappointing and unimaginative. David looks supercilious and puts my uninformed opinion down to a feminine obsession with emotions rather than technical details. The sci-fi I've read could, with fairly minor alterations, have been cowboys and Indians. Is the only difference between an imagined future and the past the difference between a laser fired from a spaceship and a Colt pistol fired from the saddle? What about life as it will be lived? What about women? They still appear as decorative props to dashing heroes. Very tedious, and they can't possibly imagine that we're going to sit back and take it right into the next century. They're more out of touch than I am, and that's not easy. It's put me off the whole sci-fi thing.

In fact women in fiction and on TV are beginning to get on my nerves. The happy housewives in the ads, hoovering houses that don't need it, smiling as they and their daughters stay at home to cook food for husbands and sons who've cleared off to the match. I saw an old sixties film recently. I know now what a sex object is. I don't want to be one any more. There were two or three actresses in the film who've since become well known. In this film they had to show their boobs and be in need of care and protection. They had to drape themselves prettily around the edges of fight scenes, looking scared, whilst all we women at home yelled 'Hit the villain with that chair, you stupid cow.' It turned me against my own sex. I don't want the girls to get the same wrong ideas. Lucy already says things like 'That lady's silly, she's awful to that man.'

Thursday 27th ☆ Cathy made a confession tonight. I was dying to hear it. She was a bit theatrical. 'Oh let's have a duty-free first.' She went to pour the drinks.

63

Then the baby stirred so she went up to settle him; 'Then we won't be disturbed later' was her excuse. She looked excited, her eyes shone. She was wearing a long loose silky affair, probably from abroad, it was the colours of jewels and patterned in large squares and lines. Cathy is beautiful and she looked her best tonight.

'It's Mr Waddington at the school,' she began eventually. 'Gareth's teacher. He ... erm ...'

'He fancies you,' I helped her out, we all know Mr Waddington, he's a dish, definitely a sex object and with an eye for the ladies.

'Right,' said Cath with a gleam in her eye. 'He's always been a bit ... well, you know how he is. When I go up to the school he'll lean over me with one arm on the wall, like this' – she stood up to show me – 'If I'm standing with my back to the wall he'll come real close and with his own arm on the wall it's as if he's shutting out the rest of the room. It makes our conversation seem intimate even if it's only about Gareth's maths. And the look in his eyes, it would melt lead.' She put her drink down on the little mat. 'Well, it was open night for Gareth's class last night so I went up to see him. He was flirty with me as he usually is but, last night, he said 'Your husband's away again, isn't he, Mrs Brooks?' I said yes, he was. So he suggested that I wait until everyone had gone and then he'd give me a lift home.' She looked at me, triumphantly?

'And did you?'

'Yes, I did. Do you think I'm awful? I enjoyed it, him flirting with me. It excited me and I felt great. We talked about York, he knows that's where I come from and he'd been there. But all the time he was talking I knew he wasn't *thinking* about York, he was thinking about me. It was wonderful, Jane, to be fancied; it's been so long.'

'Then what happened?'

'This is the awful part,' she took a sip of her drink. 'He said would I like to call in for a drink on the way back and I went.' Her face was full of guilt, triumph, joy. 'It was all above board, we went to the Crown, but Jane, I feel awful, I really enjoyed it and I didn't mention that I was pregnant. That's terrible. He's giving me a lift up to York this week-end, he has friends there. The children'll be with me of course, it'll only be a lift there on Friday night and a lift back on Monday.'

Cathy gets *awfully* lonely.

Sunday 30th ☆ It's no use trying to accept it, I can't. The fact is David's a lazy bugger and I have all the work to do. I think I'm a one-parent family.

Hope Cath hasn't done anything she'll regret or couldn't resist.

May

Monday 1st ☆ David had today off. I didn't. Told him that I was a one-parent family. He smiled. We had a quick lunch at twelve-thirty, chips and a pot of tea, a saucy little brew, vintage Co-op '78.

Lucy picked a crocus out of the garden today and came running in excitedly to show me. We went out to inspect the earth that had incredibly born fruit. I couldn't think where it had come from but I wish she'd left it alone. We would have had one flower in the garden.

Tuesday 2nd ☆ Changed nappies for pants and wet pants for dry pants and back again till my eyes crossed.

Wednesday 3nd ☆ Took Lucy to school, came home, had a cuppa with Katie, did the washing, made the beds and tidied the house, fetched Lucy home from school, cooked tea, washed up, took the children to bed, read them a story, tidied the toys away, washed up after David's meal, sat down at eight, made supper at ten and now I've come to bed, ten-fifteen.

Thursday 4th ☆ Ditto except substitute ironing for washing.

Friday 5*th* ☆ The children had to go to the dentist today – Black Friday, my nerves are in tatters. It's a huge strain to be in mortal terror on the kids' behalf and at the same time to hide it from them. I took a Valium and two headache tablets before we left, I knew I was at risk. Needn't have worried, L and K didn't need treatment, thank goodness.

Sunday 7*th* ☆ We have one solitary daffodil dropping under the weeping willow at the bottom of the garden. Mother Nature's wonderful. I've decided to give gardening one last chance and plant some lettuce seeds, although I can't see much point as lettuce will be at their cheapest by the time mine have grown.

Katie informed us at lunchtime that she's off mash. I told her that she won't grow up like Wonderwoman if she doesn't eat mash. Lucy will only eat roast potatoes and wishes I were as good as the cook in the school canteen. Times change. Neither of them will eat greens unless force fed. David asked, with distaste, if I'd bought the steak at Johnson's in the village. I said I had. 'Thought so,' he said gloomily.

'Now look,' I yelled chopping the rice pudding, 'that steak cost seventy-five pence, it's best casserole steak. So you will enjoy it, do you hear me? You Will Enjoy It!'

Wednesday 10*th* ☆ Have been writing home today, pages and pages of it. Almost as good as talking, better in a way, they can't shut me up. I was trying to cheer my father up. An old friend of his has died and it's upset him a lot, makes him conscious of his own age and mortality I suppose. My mother's letter was full of my brother and Sara, his wife, and their children. She adores Lucy and Kate, I know that, but I do feel left out. It's being away, you can't keep up with the day to day events. I feel I've grown away from my parents and I feel guilty admitting it. I love them both dearly but I don't feel they *know* me any more. But I still crave their approval and affection. My mother would never understand my wild emotions. She's so calm and organised, she'd never question what she has to do for my father, she'd never dream of it. Next time I'm home I'll ask her how she *feels* about things. I do want to know her as a person not just as a mother. I want that relationship with Lucy and Kate when they are grown up. I need my mother's unquestioning support even if I don't deserve it.

Thursday 11th ☆ Cathy behaved herself last weekend. She says she pulled herself together. When he called to pick her up, to take her home, she deliberately invited him into her parents' house for a cup of tea and, she said, how could she harbour naughty thoughts there? She says they had an intelligent conversation about her education plans and she explained to him how they would be interrupted by the birth of her fourth baby. That turned him immediately and completely off. He was polite but distant from that moment on. But it did mean that Cath's parents now know about her 'O' level. She'd been hoping to keep it secret until after her results. They laugh at her ambitions, think she's wrong in the head when she has everything she wants, nice house, husband with a good job.

Monday 15th ☆ Saw a child expert on TV this evening. She'd been blessed with a TV interview because of her startling revelation that women were missing out on the stimulating creative business of child raising by returning to interesting well-paid jobs. I used to believe that kind of thing. On the same programme they said that one in every four women will need mental treatment at some stage in their lives. The presenter seemed surprised. I was too, thought it would have been a lot more than one in four. What really shook me was that it rated TV time. Didn't know anybody cared.

I remember when I had a job, before I had the children, how I looked down on housewife friends who complained of being miserable and unhappy at home. I thought they were apathetic and ignorant. I thought they were expressing views that were fashionable rather than true. I wish I'd listened. I would have learnt so much. I really thought I'd be completely happy making dragons out of empty egg boxes all day. I really thought children were interested in dragons made of empty egg boxes. No-one ever really told me what being a wife and mother meant. I think that's wrong. I shall tell younger women the truth, if I'm ever asked. But will they believe me in the face of all those ads? They'll think me apathetic, ignorant and that I'm expressing views fashionable rather than true.

Wednesday 17th ☆ Have been looking after Gareth and Lyndsey after school today, Cathy had to go to the hospital. I made jam tarts, ready for them all coming in from school. Gareth and Lyndsey are nice. They played well with Lucy and Kate, Gareth being very gentle towards Katie. Cathy's getting a sweat on about her exam, she only has three more test papers to return to the correspondence college. She's had C's lately which has disappointed her; she wants a good grade in the exam to show her family that she's not a dizzy blonde. She has to sit the exam at the comprehensive school in Benton. If Paul isn't back, Lilian says Hugh will give her a lift in, he teaches there. Lilian isn't going to Spain for her holidays, that's common, she's going to Alicante, that's different. I could tell by the tone in her voice. She says I must sell raffle tickets to swell the carnival funds. Why didn't I just say that I have no one to sell them to? I've given them to David to sell at work. He didn't want them either.

Friday 19th ☆ Bought the ingredients for my bread-making venture at the supermarket tonight. It will have to turn out edible, I've spent so much on ingredients I can't afford to buy bread as well.

Pauline says why don't I go up to her place one night when she isn't working, we never seem to have time for a natter these days. Said I would.

Felt sorry for Janice today. They can't afford to have the bathroom done on a grant. The council only give part of the cost and insist on certain jobs being done. A friend of her husband's has offered to do it for less than it would cost on a grant. Sounds a bit suspicious to me.

Lucy's going to Sarah's party on Sunday. Think Sarah must be special because she's more than usually excited and wants to wear her silver bracelet.

Saturday, 20th ☆ Nobody told me yeast is a *living* organism, ugh. I didn't know that it grows and multiplies in warm moist conditions, but I've seen Quatermass and the Triffids and I didn't take my eyes off that basin. It frothed and it grew. It was greyish and

it bubbled. It was most definitely alive. I got it into the flour mixture at arm's length and I somehow found the resolution to mix it, knead it, and put it in the airing cupboard for a couple hours though I still don't know what that's supposed to prove. And then I forgot about it didn't I? I made the dough first thing this morning – Lilian does, and she knows, she can cure ham.

It was teatime before I remembered it. I swore and flew up the stairs, the kids ran after me, don't know what they must have thought. I flung open the airing cupboard door. We all stood back, aghast; the children's eyes were round and large. It had come up and over the rim of the mixing bowl in great billows of white, sticky, glutinous, living pulp, I fancied it was coming out to get us.

'What is it, Mummy?' breathed Lucy.

'Er ... oh ... it's a ... um,' I said with confidence and without taking my eyes off it.

They wanted to play with it, but it was hardly Play-doh. I carried it downstairs, holding it as far away from me as I could and flung it into the waste bin. I had horrors about it continuing to grow until it oozed its way out of the bin and crept across the kitchen floor to get me.

Had to race down to Johnson's then to buy a loaf. Peggy said as she served me, 'Thought you were making your own bread nowadays?' Serves me right for boasting.

Lucy piped up, 'Mummy made a big bowl of *stuff* in the airing cupboard but she threw it away.'

'*Did* she?' said Peggy and laughed.

I crawled out of the shop, one Mother's Pride tucked under my arm and two more toddling on behind.

I'll have to try again, that's my biggest headache. I've got a cupboard full of ingredients.

Sunday *21st* ☆ Poured down all day, been wandering about like a lost soul. Useless trying to get anything done when I feel like this. I go about the housework by virtue of what I'm holding in my hand. This morning I picked up the dirty coffee mugs from the bedside table, walked straight past the unmade bed and came down into the kitchen to wash them, I rinsed out the mugs and put them on the draining board, so I put away last night's washing up left to dry overnight, never entered my head to collect up the breakfast dishes and wash them. By half-past seven this morning I'd assembled two polythene kites for Lucy and Kate, getting fraught and angry because I couldn't get my struts right and by bedtime I still hadn't made the beds.

David insisted that we all walk up to the party with Lucy. He had to drag me out, I really didn't feel like facing the world, but he was right, it did do me good. I felt better whilst we were out walking, we talked a bit but I was horrid and stubborn, reluctant to meet his attempts at conversation half way. As soon as the house came into view on the way back I was depressed again, like a curtain falling across my mind. It just stood there waiting for me to clean it.

Tuesday 23rd ☆ Two days to going home time. Told Lucy and Katie today. Haven't said anything before because Lucy gets over-excited.

Lilian revealed the plans for this year's village carnival today. Lucy can be a TV character on the back of a fruit and veg lorry or an 'Ad. kid' on the back of a coal truck. She wants to be Wonderwoman. So it's the fruit and veg lorry. I shan't let Katie take part, the imagination curdles at the thought of what Katie could do given the free run of a lofty moving vehicle.

Thursday 25th ☆ On films, people who are packing simply go to wardrobes and drawers and pull out heaps of clean ironed clothes and stuff them into suitcases. You never see them grubbing round in the laundry basket for things they haven't washed. It's not worth it, it's just not worth it for a few days at home. All this extra work and anguish and it's bound to make us overdrawn. I'm knackered – but then, as I said to Katie, we'll be sleeping at Grandma's tomorrow night. It will be worth it then. I've been repeating it all day to keep myself going.

Friday, 26th ☆ We're here. It's heaven. All my cares dropped away as I stepped through the door and flopped out on that beautiful familiar tatty old settee. I feel a thousand miles away from Blackthorne Bridge. I can't remember the last time I felt so relaxed. Bliss.

Mum and Dad were in the window watching for us as Lucy had predicted. She stood all the way, more than two hundred miles, not wanting to miss seeing the Yorkshire boundary. We all cheer when we reach it.

I enjoy being driven in the car. The kids *have* to stay in the back, not because mummy's sick and tired of them climbing on her but for their own safety, so I can feel virtuous as well as have my body to myself.

Feel sure you can't get done for potty stops on the hard shoulder. David isn't. He was annoyed, but when they've gotta go they've gotta go.

Dad looks a lot better, says it's due to his new tablets. Mum looks very tired. She says it's the worry over my father. I feel worried about her.

Going to my brother's tomorrow, dying to see them all.

Saturday 27th ☆ Great day. Lucy and Kate are sleeping at Sara's, my sister-in-law's, they didn't want to leave their cousins. I've kept coming upstairs quietly, can't get used to them not being here. David's been out for a pint with Simon, my brother, and Dad tonight. He's enjoyed that. He misses old times too, and Yorkshire brewed beer. I could have gone, I could have gone, incredible, the freedom. Didn't want to, too tired and I didn't get up till nine. The kids woke mum and she brought them down and fed them according to Lucy's instructions. She washed Katie's nappies too. Every time there's mention of a cup of tea I automatically get up to make it, and Mum shoos me back down and she makes it. She has enough to do, but says she wants me to have a real break and I'm looking thin and pale. Imagine anyone noticing, could only be my mum, though Sara did too. She said, 'You look awfully pale and tired Jane. Is David helping you?' I said not much. 'He should,' she said, 'it's hard going when they're little like Lucy and Kate. I'll have a word with him.' She looked determined but I don't know if she has. I think it was probably Sara's doing that the girls have stayed there tonight, she brainwashed them into thinking it was a good idea. She's thoughtful.

Am eating like a horse here, thank goodness, I do worry about my lack of appetite. Didn't tell mum about the Valium.

Sunday 28th ✩ I'm so sleepy all the time, seeing everything through a haze. Don't like it, want to savour every precious minute. Went to spend the day with David's parents today. D's dad still working on the farm in his spare time. D's mum told me with a look that she's fed-up with it. D's brothers are fine, chasing girls and boozing, D spent hours inspecting their motor bikes, envying them. It's what he'd have if he didn't have a wife and kids.

So many people to keep an eye on Katie, she doesn't seem nearly so wild.

Didn't have time to go and see Diana and Nick, our old friends. Sad about that.

75

Monday 29th ☆ Back again, say no more. Acutely aware of the home me and the here me. Things don't get to me at home as they do here. I'm more relaxed. Maybe I'm just a square peg in a round hole here, Blackthorne Bridge isn't home to me.

Tuesday 30th ☆ What a difference no overtime makes. David comes home at half-past five now so we can all fight at meal times instead of just me and the kids. David is furious if either of them fails to eat everything. 'There's children starving in India,' he yells. It's what his mother used to say to him. I hate those hours from half-past four until half-past seven when the children go to bed. Seem to cram a day's work into three hours.

The trousers Sara gave me fit, more or less. Feel fashionable because they're air-force blue.

June

Thursday 1st ☆ Fifteen pounds overdrawn last month, trip home and five Fridays. Either our bank manager is a nice guy or the interest charges on our overdraft are keeping the minimum lending rate down. The weather is good. Lucy pulled the paddling pool out today. Katie toddled about playing with sand and water and weeing on everything. Warned her off my lettuce. Can't remember exactly where they are.

Lilian called about the carnival. David sold all the raffle tickets so she's supplied me with another bookful. This time I said no, I'd no one to sell them to and we'd sold a lot for her. I'm always stronger and braver after a visit home. She said, 'Oh, come on Jane, if everyone took that attitude we'd never raise enough money. You could go up to the new estate or what about the school?'

The new estate will have been covered so will the school and anyway why didn't I just say no? What if they *don't* raise enough money? It won't be the end of my world. But I didn't say it, I accepted the tickets and said I'd try. She wouldn't argue if I was a strong person, she would accept defeat but she knows I'm weak and manageable.

But something's dawning in my mind. I'm quite wrong about myself. I'm *not* a weak person who must try and become strong. I am fundamentally a strong, opinionated person but I've trained myself to appear

77

weak because that's how I'm supposed to be. Strong, opinionated women aren't nice. I must get this straight in my mind. I've tried to be 'less', less than a man, less than any man in my life, father, brother, boyfriend, husband, less strong emotionally, less clever, less funny. Everybody knows that's how it should be, men and women alike and including me. I like men to be men, to be 'more' than me, but they so often aren't. I can even see now why I failed at school. There was a sense almost of disappointment in my parents when it was me who began to do well in school and not my brother, who was older. Faint disappointment and barely perceptible, but it was there. They did encourage me but – I could never quite exult in my little achievements, felt they should have been my brother's. The idea that I'm not 'less' must have crept up on me slowly and without me knowing. And as it did, just as unconsciously, I grew a skin over it, I tried to ignore it. But there's no denying one's self, it's a terrible mistake. I will simply *have* to be me. 'They' must take me or leave me alone, and I must accept that. Would David notice the change? And if so, would he be a taker or a leaver?

My brother is the sales manager for a big company now. Could I have been?

Saturday 3rd ☆ Had a good weep this evening. David and I were reading, mine was a whodunnit, but I couldn't get into it, the characters were like cardboard. The radio was on and a woman began to sing 'Sailing', the Rod Stewart song, and I wept and wept. David asked me what was the matter. 'I love you.' I said, 'I love Lucy and Kate. I want to hold them in my arms and never let them go. I want to give them the moon and the stars but I shout at them and I love them.'

78

He made me a cup of tea dnd tried to console me. 'You're not so bad in the summer,' he said.

Monday 5*th* ☆ Mrs Jenkins and Ernest are to be wed on the first of July and the four of us are invited. It's to be at the village church and the reception will be at the village hall, vandals permitting. They look so happy, Mrs J and Ernest, like a pair of teenagers. Mrs J brought a bag of her granddaughter's outgrown clothes, thought they might come in useful for Lucy and Kate. They will.

Still no luck on the potty.

Tuesday 6*th* ☆ Tackled the bread situation again today, turned out better than last time. This batch got as far as the oven.

David came home all eager and watering at the mouth for his promised home-made bread. 'What's that evil smell?' he said.

'It's the bread,' I said.

'Good God,' he said.

It had a greyish tinge and the internal consistency of a crumpet. David picked up the bread knife. 'You're not going to eat it?' I gasped.

'Give it a go,' he said with loyalty and great courage.

We all stood about anxiously watching him chew – and chew.

'It's not all that good,' he said, but he swallowed it. 'Never mind, love,' he flung an arm round my shoulders. 'You did try.'

'I can't do a bloody thing right,' I said slapping the table with the tea towel.

'Course you can,' he said. 'I'll never forget that sponge you made.'

'What sponge?'

'Don't you remember? When my parents were coming for tea that time.'

'The first time.' I said, 'We were just married, it was ten years ago.'

Still got some ingredients left.

Wednesday 7th ☆ When we woke up this morning the air was clear and bright. The sun was shining and the birds were singing. It was as if summer had come. I asked David to miss work for once, say he was sick or something, and take us all to the coast.

'I can't do that,' he said.

Heigh ho heigh ho it's off to work we go. I wish Lil had told me about all those lazy British workmen who spend their time on strike or the dole before I married David. I'd have married one of them instead, you're never alone with a drone.

Thursday 8th ☆ Excitement, excitement, prospects of change in the Bennett household *and* Cathy did her exam today and all went well.

David's seriously thinking of applying for a job he's seen advertised in the paper. It's a big decision because he's fairly secure in his present job, farm machines will always need maintaining and repairing, and security is worth the world these days. Kenny's still out of work.

This new job is with a Swedish company opening up a UK factory on the industrial estate they've built on the other side of Benton. They manufacture plastic things for kitchens, dish drainers etc., and they want a production supervisor. A company car, a telephone and a lot more money go with the job. David's excited and nervous about it. He's got an application form.

Pauline's been to visit her newly married cousin and is definitely off her new cousin-in-law. 'Do you know what he said?' She was horrified. 'She made some tea, sugared and stirred *his*, carried it to him in the living room, *he* didn't move out of his armchair all the time I was there, he took a sip, pulled a face and asked her what she'd done to it, said it didn't taste right. I mean a cup of tea is a cup of tea.'

'What did she do?' I asked.

'Silly cow, she said "sorry love" took the cup off him and made a fresh pot. I'd have crowned him with it.'

Felt like Slack Alice in Johnson's shop today, all the women with their suntans and pretty summery clothes.

Friday 9th ☆ The girls are buying a photograph frame for Mrs J and Ernest. A good idea, it was Lilian's. Cathy's growing, we've been trying to decipher the medical jargon on her clinic card today but we can't. She has this dreadful pain in her right thigh and we thought the card might have given a clue as to what was causing it. Pauline said it would be the baby laying on a nerve but I'd always understood that there weren't any nerves in the womb. We'll never know, you never do find out anything. Cathy has terrible heartburn too, it wakes her up all the time. They've given her the white chalky stuff for it. It works sometimes but the only cure is to have the baby. Being pregnant is bloody awful.

Lucy is going to Edward-like-the-prince's (Lilian's son) birthday party tomorrow. He's ten.

Took our coffee into the garden this evening and sat with the children. Too nice for the supermarket. We're going to do David's application form tonight. If he gets this job he'll never want to go home to Yorkshire.

81

Don't know what I can buy for Edward's birthday, he's got everything.

Saturday 10th ☆ Been to Edward's party with Lucy. Lilian asked me to stay, so I did. The house was crawling with people, Lilian and Hugh's friends and relations all making much of Martyn — a doting Aunthill. It was awful, cloying and I wish my kids came in for a bit more spoiling and petting.

Could sense a tinge of rivalry between Lilian and her two sisters. I commented on the magnificent abundance of food, how nice it all looked, Lilian said she couldn't have done it without her deep-freezer. The two sisters murmured agreement. 'Oh yes,' said one, 'I remember when Laurence got engaged, we had sixty guests,' she gave a little coy laugh, 'Oh I'd *never* have coped without my deep-freeze.'

'Don't you remember my mother-in-law's golden wedding?' said the other. 'I made the cake *weeks* before the event. We had eighty to that.' She fingered her pearls. They're nice enough women, spreading hips as they approach middle age, not as chic as Lilian who benefits from her mother-in-law's guiding hand. Her sisters were wearing chain store dresses in horrible colours and fabrics, hot pink and shiny was one. They're complacent and content with their lives and deep freezers. I felt out of place, nervy, wanted to be one of them for Lucy's sake. She had a ball, unused to so many toys. There's a climbing frame in the garden that Kate would give an arm for, two swings, a slide and a paddling pool that would accommodate Moby Dick. But there were no parcels to pass or donkeys to pin tails on. The children, about fifteen of them, had tea first, all home made stuff of course, cake like a treasure island, 'X' marked the spot and Edward dug out a couple of chocolate doubloons. Lucy was quiet at the poshness of it all, so I stood with my hands on the back of her chair for moral support. Felt that eating a cake before at least three sandwiches would mean six lashes. The men ate next and then we women ate what everyone else had spurned. Not stricly true. Lilian had kept a fresh cream gateau for us. All I wanted was a fag and a cup of coffee but didn't dare ask so drank tea and listened to talk about people I didn't know.

I met Lilian's mother for the first time, in the hall, that's where we'd both escaped for a crafty drag. She's a not very tall, very ordinary, working-class woman. My heart warmed to her. She's overweight, quite a lot overweight, and her hair had been cut too short before perming. She'd obviously had it done for Edward's party and the set was too fixed and severe. She was shy and self-conscious. I felt, and I'm afraid she did too, that she was being ever so slightly shunned by her children. She'd tried to dress smartly for Lilian, I could see that, and she tried to speak nicely too, but she was no match for Hugh's elegant mother. She seemed hesitant with Edward as if she wasn't quite good enough to be his Gran. I ached to tell her that I understood but there was no way I could, and I may be wrong.

Don't think Hugh does wear suspenders on his socks as Pauline and I thought likely, had a sneaky look while he and I were talking in the garden. He's proud of his marrows and said they were very sexy plants – imagine Hugh saying *that* word, what is the world coming to – because you need a male and a female. I said if the marrows grew crooked did it mean the parent plants had been bent? *And* he knew what I meant. Wonder if Lilian knows what a little raver lies beneath his bi-focals?

Bought a Mastermind game for Edward, he's sure to be.

David looked tense when we got back. 'Katie wees ...' he said, shoulders hunched, arms spread, hands moving in despairing circles, eyes looking wildly round the room, 'everywhere.'

Tuesday 13th ✩ I always thought watching Wimbledon was a perk for stay-at-home wives − I was wrong. Perhaps I can train them into a subdued silence before Finals day. I've tried everything. 'If you don't speak for five minutes I'll give you a biscuit ... if you'll go out to play I'll buy you some chocolate tomorrow.' Doesn't help.

Katie is sleeping better (which means longer) these days, fresh air and exercise. Think I'll buy her a treadmill for Christmas. The weather is great, everyone going without tights, except me with my whiter-shade-than-pale skin. Lil has terrible varicose veins, I noticed them today although she wears thick stockings. She says they play up in this hot weather. I don't think she should be taking the pill with those veins. 'I don't suppose I'll have to for much longer,' she said with a wry smile. I took her to mean she's getting near menopause. I didn't think she was as old as that. I told her to see the doctor about her veins but she said 'Huh, doctors.'

We're going to have to buy clothes for Mrs J's wedding. David can wear his suit but the children and I have nothing remotely suitable. Lucy can't wear the dress she wears to parties. There'll be photographs and everyone will notice. We'll have to go to Norwich on Saturday. It's probably too late to order from Pauline's catalogue. Once I've reasoned away the horror at what it's all going to cost, I shall look forward to the trip.

Thinking of china for a wedding present. Mrs J likes china, will have to be something special, a delicate chamber pot for cold winter nights? She says she won't be having any more of them – cheeky little devil.

Wednesday 14th ☆ Have ordered myself a dress from Pauline's catalogue. We posted the order off straight away with 'urgent' scrawled over it. The catalogue was full of prettier, cheaper dresses but all designed to be worn without a bra. Everyone must be doing it if it's hit the mail order books. I couldn't go bra-less. Could I? No, I fed the children with them. Mine aren't decorative, they've been useful.

Thursday 15th ☆ Searched in vain for my cleavage after my bath tonight. It's slipped down my chest

85

someplace with my poor little boobs. Oh *why* don't I look like Raquel Welch?

Lilian says I should smack Katie when she wets herself. I can't do that, the man in the mag. says it leads to hang ups in later life, anyway it's cruel. But what if it worked?

Saturday 17th ☆ Exhausting, expensive day in Norwich yesterday. Am pleased with the wedding present, found a boxed gift set of a pair of Wedgwood cups and saucers. Think she'll like them but won't use them. Spent the best part of fifty pounds altogether, I feel sick when I think of the end of this month. We'll never be financially straight again.

Had an angry exchange with David after tea today – nothing so passion-filled as a full blown row in this house. He wanders away as if he's afraid of them. He just opts out of being part of the family. When we came back from Norwich yesterday he collapsed on the settee. Today all I wanted was for him to keep Katie out of the way, but he wouldn't, he had to wash the car and no way would he let Katie within five yards of the hose pipe. It's a wise father that knows his own child. I was trying to finish Lucy's costume for the carnival and was on pins trying to keep Katie away from same, and Lucy went off the idea of being Wonderwoman and I bent my bullet deflectors and the carrots burnt over and I boiled over and David said why hadn't I said she'd be an Oxo cube in a painted cardboard box like last year. I said if he spent more time talking to his children he'd know why and that he didn't take his share of responsibility. He said what did I want him to do, play happy families? And why did I think he worked so hard if he wasn't aware of his responsibilities.

We haven't spoken to each other all evening so that's passed off as usual but he's gone to sleep without saying goodnight and you should never let the sun set on your wrath. You should stay up and fight. He's got an interview for that job tomorrow, I expect he's edgy about it. I haven't helped him, but he hasn't helped me either.

Sunday 18th ☆ Why do I constantly fail to live up to my standards of mothering? Are they my standards? Or are they set by the learned who are not, so to speak, in the front line of the battle with all the muck and the bullets. Why do I get so irritable? Because I've run out of Valium. Why do I need Valium? To numb my rebelling mind into insensibility? Why should I need to numb it, isn't it like an arm or a leg, if you don't use it for long enough it will eventually drop off? Why am I a failure? Because I'm not cut-out for this line of work. Because I didn't realise that motherhood comes neat.

Monday 19th ☆ David's been shortlisted, thrilled to bits, couldn't wipe the grin off his face. He hurried in through the kitchen door, a great grin on his face, I haven't seen him like it for ages. He picked Katie up and swung her in the air, she squeaked in delight. I've pressed his suit again, he has to go to the Three Feathers on Wednesday night. D thinks there are two others on the short list for his job and that they're choosing a general manager on Wednesday too. I'm disloyal, I have mixed feelings about this new job. I hope for his sake that he gets it but *if* he does I know he won't consider going back home and I also know that the work will keep him away from us even more.

Lucy brought a note home from school about the annual outing. They're going to Seacombe, it's going to cost about seven pounds and that's not counting what they'll spend when they're there. She's so excited, how can I say that we can't afford it?

Tuesday 20th ☆ 'David,' I began, hesitantly, 'about this new job.' He was in the armchair watching TV, but he turned to face me immediately. His mind hadn't been on the programme. I tried to smile but it was weak and feeble, I know how much the job means to him. His face as it turned to me was radiant, smiling. It was all there written in his features, the hope, the good things in store, the step up the ladder and the pride and satisfaction that that would bring. How could I say what I wanted to say. I *knew* how he felt without asking.

'Well,' he said, still smiling. 'Do you want a fur coat out of the pay rise?' He laughed fondly. I smiled.

'It's about going home David, the five years, they're up in October.'

His face dropped, it crashed, transformation. 'What do you mean?'

'We won't be going back home to Yorkshire then. You want to stay here forever.' I tried to make it light. At that moment I really didn't *know* if it was best to go home or stay here. I was completely confused, torn in two by my interests and David's.

'Jane. Love.' He came over and knelt beside my chair putting his hands on my shoulders, looking into my face. 'If I get this job we'd be mad to go back to Yorkshire.'

I burst into tears, because we couldn't go home, because it wasn't right that we should go home, because a job for David is important it governs how we all live, because I'll never be right while we live here, this isn't home to me.

He sat on the arm of my chair, his arms around me. 'I don't think going home would cure your troubles, Jane,' his voice was soothing. 'I know being stuck in the house gets you down. I talked to Sara about it at Whitsun, she made me promise I'd help you more. I know I haven't but I will Jane, I will. I've been down as well, Jane, I haven't felt like helping. I can't take you out, we've never any money, I can't buy you clothes and things. It will be different if I get this job, we'll have a new car, a company car, we won't be worrying about breakdowns and repairs and paying for them and there'll be no tax and insurance to find. And we'll have a telephone, you'll be able to phone your mother and Sara if you feel down. We'll have a lot more money, we'll be going out, having holidays, you'll be able to go into Norwich shopping, all things like that. It will be a whole new life, you'll be much happier. If we went back I'd be unemployed, we'd be as badly off there as we are here and I don't believe just being in Yorkshire would make up for that.'

I was content to believe him, it was better than confusion.

'And if you don't get the job?'

'If I don't get the job, we'll talk about going back.'

Wednesday 21st ☆ He's been and he's back and he still doesn't know. He's had supper and several drinks and feels hopeful because the bosses seemed to talk to him a lot. They'll let him know by letter in the next few days. He's keener than ever to get it.

Thursday 22nd ☆ Teatime, the three of them were

sitting round the table, I was at the stove. Lucy was shouting that Katie had pinched her knife and fork, Katie was yelling for a drink of juice, David's voice droned on about the new job. Suddenly I saw them all as three huge, gaping mouths that could only demand, demand, demand, time, attention, food, drink, explanation, care and protection. I bellowed at them to shut up. There was a sudden stunned silence. How do other women cope?

I vanished to Cathy's as soon as the kids were in bed. What did I do before we had our Thursday nights? I started to tell Cath about David's job etc but I had to stop because Pauline came. Poor lass, Kenny's still out and no prospect of work. I could hardly talk about D's possible good fortune in the circs. She looked grey, says she doesn't know how they'll manage. Kenny says he's going to go into business with his brother, a jobbing builder. Pauline hates Kenny's brother, says he's a shyster, he'd swindle his own mother.

Saturday 24th ☆ Village carnival today and it drizzled. Was worried about Lucy catching cold in her costume. She was thrilled with it. I walked along beside the lorry, David walked with Katie who whizzed around in small circles yelling 'wonderwooman'.

Lilian thoroughly enjoyed herself being frantic because the draperies fell off the Carnival Queen's float and no one could come up with a drawing pin. Saw Pauline and Kenny glaring at each other over the heads of the girls. Cathy was there with offspring *and* Paul. Saw Mrs Jenkins and Ernest arm-in-arm, David made masculine jokes with Ernest, Mrs J laughed a lot and bought ice-cream for Lucy and Kate. I wanted balloons and giant lollipops and to win a goldfish for them but we hadn't any money.

Lucy's float came second, one from the new estate got first prize, sweets all round.

Lucy and Katie should sleep tonight please God – I did say please.

Monday 26th ☆ David's got the job. They want him to start after our holidays. He has to go on a training course for a week in Nottingham. He's in a state of bliss.

Thursday 29th ☆ Have made the supreme sacrifice and been on the school outing. It wasn't so bad, the weather was warm and sunny so Pauline, Cathy, the eight children and myself spent most of the day cheaply on the beach, sitting on the sand among broken beer bottles and fag ends, eyeing up the talent. Pauline said, 'Ooh, I could *murder* a tall blond beach boy.'

I was a bit late getting to the bus this morning so they jeered when we arrived. It annoys me, they behave as if I'm always late and I'm not, not always. We all took picnics. Cathy had bread rolls spread with butter and stuffed with salad and cold meat, packed in linen napkins and neat plastic boxes. Pauline and I had sliced bread spread with marge and stuffed with paste, packed in plastic loaf bags. Cathy looked as clean and neat and lovely coming home as she did going. I was harassed and sticky before the driver turned the ignition key this morning. I wore my air-force blue trousers from Sara. They looked all right.

Friday 30th ☆ Been to Mrs J's for a pre-nuptial knees-up with the ladies of the Over-Sixties club.

Carla, her daughter-in-law, and I were in the drunks corner swilling port and lemon and smiling at all the old ladies belting out 'I'm getting married in the morning.' Mrs J passed between the groups and the trays of meat pies with bottles of port and laughing replies to all the teasing she came in for. Old age pensioners can be positively wanton.

This time tomorrow it will all be over.

July

Saturday 1st ☆ The bells have rung for Ernest and his gal. The birds have sung, the sun has shone, the roses have blossomed and bloomed. Even Katie was reasonably tame.

Ernest and his best man stood like ramrods with just the occasional glance at their pocket watches, stiff white collars cutting into their ruddy men's necks.

Geoff gave his Mum away. It was all very dignified, so much more meaning somehow than when youngsters rush into they know not what – like what we did.

Mrs J wore powder blue, a matching dress and coat in an unpatterned fabric, and a hat trimmed with pale blue feathers. Her pearls were around her neck, an orchid corsage, a present from Ernest, pinned to her coat and she carried a prayer book to which she'd pinned the other orchid corsage, a present from Carla and Geoff.

All the village turned out to watch. Lilian said I looked very nice – there's a plum for me.

The best man had obviously put a lot of thought into his speech. It was really quite good – not rude. He read the cards – some of which were rude – and the telegram from Ernest's son in South Africa. The toasts were drunk, the cake was cut and Rosie and Ernest left for their secret honeymoon in Seacombe in a shower of confetti.

Carla and I sat at a table in the corner and leant on our elbows eating meat pies and drinking dark brown tea that made my head ache from thick white cups. We both said how nice it was for Mrs J and Ernest to have found companionship in their old age, and it is, but I had this fleeting thought about the disruption to Mrs J's quiet life, she'll have another to please and clear up after.

I wish I could have a good wife – it must be heaven.

Sunday 2nd ✩ Thought I'd make like a good wife today, try the role for size so to speak, so when the kids woke me at seven I got up. I didn't speak – judging it to be the safest course if I was to sustain the smiling madonna mask.

When I emerged from the bedroom and saw that Katie had crayonned up the stair wall, thickly and in orange, I did not immediately screech and scream. I led her by the hand to the scene of her crime and then I screeched and screamed.

Have been reading the novels of Alexander Kent lately so that I'll have something to talk to David about. I'm not the kind of person who gives up easily. He has a current passion for Alexander Kent and his hero the dashing Capt. Bolitho. He's reading his way through all that the library can supply. I'll be joining him in that, I'm enjoying them. They're swashbuckling stories of the Royal Navy around the time of the American War of Independence. David obviously identifies with the dashing Rich Bolitho and so do I but I fancy him like mad as well – all that power and command – lovely. I can see myself pacing the quarterdeck issuing crisp, executive commands. I'd be ice cool but diabolically clever in battle, lead my adoring crew to victory – like Mrs Thatcher – and have a man in every port – unlike Mrs Thatcher (I would think). Not that Capt. Bolitho sullies himself with sex – it wouldn't be cricket chaps – he doesn't seem to indulge but that's because he never met me, fine spirited wench with a rump ripe for slapping.

I read to escape.

Tuesday 4th ☆ I keep turning back to my entry of June 1st, I re-read it. If I peel off this 'skin' and find myself, if I begin to behave with the heart and mind God gave me, what will happen? Will I overpower my husband, my friends? I'm frightened that I may. Would I be too much? I love David, other men seem petty by comparison. But is he as strong as I could be? It worries me, it worries me too much to test it.

I'll leave the skin in place, the corner I've scratched will heal over. It's better that way.

Wednesday 5th ☆ Had a letter from Diana and Nick, can they come down for August Bank Holiday? Have written straight back to say yes.

Cathy's next door neighbour's little boy has the German measles. Cath is past the dangerous period but she's naturally worried and she's not sure if she can have tests or anything done about it now.

Saturday 22nd ☆ Where to begin? What a fortnight. We've been home and now we're back. My mother is well again, she's had a heart attack but she's OK now, still in hospital but not for much longer. We arrived back home this evening, thank God David has the next two weeks off. I feel like a dish rag. I can't stop worrying about my mother.

When the telegram came my heart stopped, didn't think it would ever start again. Lilian was wonderful. I must go and thank her tomorrow.

It was the last Friday of term, whatever date that was, I've lost all track of time. I'd gone to the shop, Katie was with me and Lilian was there, we were talking to Peggy. Steven, the postman, saw me there and brought the telegram in to me, the blessings of village life. My hands were shaking, out of all control, my head was full of whirling thoughts of my father, never dreamt it could be my mother. I must have been ashen. I passed the telegram to Lilian, still trembling so that the paper shook. I didn't know what to do, I was helpless, no telephone, Lucy in school, David at work. Lilian said we'd better go to her place straight away. She's on the phone and we could ring David's boss from there. Lilian put Katie in the back of her car, I shoved my shopping into my bag, I think Lilian paid for it, I was completely dazed. She took Katie to play in her back garden and sat me on a chair in the hall with a glass of whisky. She phoned David's boss and I heard her say, 'Then you'd better get him back from Webster's Farm NOW.' Everyone obeys Lilian. David seemed to be there almost at once. We picked Lucy up from school, threw clothes into a suitcase, coffee into a flask and left for home.

We went straight to the hospital. She was still in intensive care, but was already improving, crisis over when we got there. But I couldn't help thinking of what might have been. What if she'd died before I got there? Before I'd seen her?

Sunday 23rd ☆ Walked up to Lilian's after lunch today. Lucy and Kate played in the garden with Edward. The four of us sat in the spotless comfortable

97

lounge, drinking tea from fine china cups laid out on a low table and watched the children play through the open patio doors. It was relaxing and peaceful after the strain of the last couple of weeks.

Lilian waved away our thanks, said it was only what anyone would have done. They've invited us to supper next Saturday. Hugh says he promises not to bore us with a single word about the people they met on holiday if we refrain from telling him the various roads we take to drive to Yorkshire. I'm surprised to have things in common with Hugh.

Wish we could have patio doors.

Monday 24th ☆ Busy in the house all day, result of a fortnight away. Lucy and Kate played out, pleased to be home with their toys. David cleaned the windows under duress so they're worse now than they were but full marks for trying – he's a different man since he got this new job, more cheerful, brighter, it makes me feel good. He officially left the garage last Friday.

Went to Pauline's this evening, they'd been having words. I could tell, you didn't need to be Sherlock Holmes. He sat at one end of the room and she sat at the other. Kenny remarked 'Turned chilly tonight, Jane.' Pauline snarled, 'Not so chilly that you want to stay in though, is it?' Kenny said, mildly, to make sure he got right under her skin, 'Well, Jane's come out in the cold night air, love.'

Pauline controlled herself but I don't know how, she was livid. I didn't know what to do so I stayed where I was perched on the fluffy yellow seat cushion, which always reminds me of teddy bears, in the black vinyl armchair, my eyes swivelling from one to the other like a spectator at Wimbledon.

Eventually Pauline offered Kenny a pound to clear

off up the Crown but only if he'd make us some tea first. He jumped at the chance and provided a plate of biscuits as well as two mugs of tea. He asked 'Do you want a Nice biscuit, love?' Pronouncing Nice as 'nice' instead of 'niece'. Pauline was ready to explode.

He'd seemed embarrassed at obeying his wife in front of me. Pauline says he wasn't embarrassed, he was secretly thrilled at the opportunity of showing me what he has to put up with and the saintly way he does it. She said he'd been hankering after going out for a drink all night and he'd been on pins wondering how he could get round her for a pound because he's skint. You'd think he'd want to stay in with her, wouldn't you, kid? With all the moaning he does about her being out five nights a week working at the bingo hall. She feels like leaving home.

She cheered up after he'd gone, as if she'd dismissed the argument from her mind. But she hadn't. It was only half-time. We looked at her catalogue and wanted most of what was in it, I paid my dues for the dress, we had a laugh over things the kids had said and done. She says Cathy is quite well but looked exhausted when she left and that if she were Cathy and expecting her fourth she's put her head in the gas oven. Cath should be getting her exam result before long, do hope she's done well. She and the children have gone to her mother's for the holidays. Paul is abroad. Pauline says she had to laugh at Cath, she had so much preparing to do for the trip she kept saying, 'Oh, I'll be all right once I get this holiday over with.'

We sat on the red, orange and brown swirly patterned foam-backed carpet, our eyes drawn from time to time to the gigantic colour telly. Next door they were watching a western, I could hear it through the walls. The curtains are orange imitation velvet and the walls are anaglypta emulsioned orange and white

99

alternately. Tends to make the eyes cross. There's a painting above the fireplace of a small boy with a large tear sliding down his cheek. It always reminds me of Katie.

When Kenny came back, about a quarter past eleven, he offered to walk me home. Pauline snapped, 'Oh yes,' then in a false voice, fawning, in sarcastic imitation of Kenny she said, 'You can't walk home on your own Jane, not in the dark Jane, let big gentleman Kenny escort you Jane. Only don't count on him protecting you kid,' – the last in her normal voice, 'not if you're mugged or something. You'll have to look after him.'

I thought it best to decline his offer.

Family life is wonderful when everyone else is in bed. I am on my holidays.

Wednesday 26th ☆ Had a brainwave today. It rained, so we took the children to the airport. Had a great time and goose pimples at every take-off and landing, there were only three but I made everyone count telling Lucy and Kate all about foreign countries etc. Wish it had been fine enough to go out on to the spectator's gallery, but the trip was a success. We're going again. Saw Mr Waddington flying out to Spain with a tall brunette. I'd love to go abroad, anywhere, but I'd especially like to take the girls to Disneyland.

Thursday 27th ☆ Been to the library. They're going to have story-reading sessions during the school holidays. Had a stroll around Benton, bought cards for Mum's birthday and wedding anniversary. Walking round Benton was quite different today, I felt relaxed and happy, perhaps because David was with us, perhaps because I wasn't dashing to get Lucy from school or worrying about the times of buses.

Friday 28th ☆ This is Leighton your milkman called. Worked out the bill for him, he trusts me. Seven days at three pints, fifteen days (when David was here on his own and we were in Yorks) at one pint followed by six days at three pints was just too much, his eyes were crossing trying to follow his ready reckoner, he doesn't understand it anyway and we'd have been passing thirty-four pences back and forward all night.

Mrs J and Ernest will be glad to sit on Lucy and Kate for us tomorrow night.

Took the kids swimming this afternoon, which was brave of me because I'm desperately ashamed of showing my legs and their purple veins. I ran from the changing rooms so as to hide them in the water. Wish the pool was easier to get to, I could take Katie during the day then. Both girls loved it.

Saturday 29th ☆ Been to supper with Lilian and Hugh, enjoyed being out but got a bit bored. Lilian was so quiet, she leaves the field clear for Hugh. She just sat there, listening, not at all like she is with us women. Hugh and David nattered on about UFOs and strange lines on the land of Latin American countries and the Bermuda Triangle. I kept butting in, dying to talk about my theories, but D and H didn't want theories, they kept repeating the facts they'd read. Felt silly, like an over-exuberant teenager. When they moved on to Hugh's new car, I couldn't join in, so I tried to content myself with the food – ate like a horse. Lilian said she never knew I ate so much, how did I keep so thin? I said I only eat other people's food, never what I cooked myself, which is true but I don't think she believed me. Wore my new dress, felt matronly in it.

They played records by the Carpenters. Had been half expecting fugues and opuses.

Sunday 30th ☆ Slammed the washing machine round the kitchen in a rage singing 'This is my holiday, it is the day I shall remember the day I'm dying.' David hoovered through the house. I think the two are connected.

Monday 31st ☆ Went to the Forest Centre this afternoon. Marvellous place to take the children, not an ice-cream vendor in miles. Several stopping places with commando-type climbing nets, tyre swings, tree trunk forts, log cabins and so on. I couldn't have coped without David, but without his proud encouragement the kids may not have attempted the terrifying feats they did. He told me to stop worrying, they were all right and I should have seen some of the things he did as a lad. We took a picnic lunch, what else? We ate it on a rustic bench with the flies and ants. Katie weed in her pants at each stopping place. Think she could bring life to the Sahara.

This time next week David will be in Nottingham starting his course.

August

Tuesday 1st ☆ Happy birthday Mum. Kids slept till half-past seven, thanks to yesterday's activities. *Must* go again.

In the garden today – pottering. David didn't want to join me, he says it makes you blind. He found what could loosely be described as lettuce, gone to seed. We can't eat it. Mowed the lawns, that's how we found the lettuce. David washed the car, he's found a buyer, a chap who goes to the Crown. *Four hundred pounds*, we're going to have four hundred pounds in the bank and a whole lot of arguments about how it's to be spent. Could spend it now on clothes and the house. Four hundred isn't enough to buy all the clothes and everything we need for the house. David wants to save it for a proper holiday next year and we'd get the interest on a year's savings. I agree that's what we should do, but I don't know if I can wait that long. Anyway, shouldn't count our chickens before they're hatched, the man hasn't made his mind up for sure yet.

Lucy found a red plastic milk crate and dragged it up the path with a huge smile on her face. 'Look Mum,' she said, 'it's for you. The milkbottles won't fall down and break now.' I was deeply touched.

Thursday 3rd ☆ Out all day, beach and airport,

picnic lunch and tea. I *must* be turning a honeyed hue by now, I've just got to be.

David went up the Crown for a drink, didn't see the man about the car but it was as good an excuse as any for going.

Finished last month ten pounds overdrawn, which is something of a miracle in view of all the to-ing and fro-ing we had to do to Yorks. If we can sell the car it will end all our money troubles even without David's new job. He's right – money is the root of all my evils, just the thought of four hundred in the bank lightens my heart.

This time next week I shall have spent four David-less nights and four David-less days.

Friday 4th ☆ Letter from Cathy, she's fed-up to the teeth. If Paul wasn't due to join her she'd pack up and come home. Her mother doesn't know what she was thinking of getting herself pregnant again. Her sister-in-law claims that her kids don't get away with half of what Cathy's kids do.

Sunday 6th ☆ He's gone. Left around three this afternoon. 'Be careful on the roads,' I said. We haven't spent all that money on fags for him to kill himself in the car.

What if someone breaks in? How will I get to the children undetected? If the mad axe-man doesn't come and rape me tonight all will be well, a safe first night will be an omen. Daren't look in the mirror in case someone lurks behind me. Can't help seeing it from here, will force myself to look, no I won't, I'll read myself to sleep. Chose these library books very carefully, no sex or violence, can't have the former and don't want the latter till David comes home.

Monday 7th ☆ Glorious day, mad axe-man didn't come, fuses didn't blow. Wonder how David is? Wonder if he's eaten all his chocolate. I hid walnut whips in his Y-fronts and clean shirts, they're his favourite. Wonder if he's missing me?

Did the washing, sunbathed in the garden with the kids. Felt free somehow, and incredibly lazy.

Tuesday 8th ☆ Am enjoying my solitary bedtimes, think I'm sinful but I can read for as long as I like and eat in bed. Wish the library would change their filing system, they arrange the fiction alphabetically according to the authors' names. I wish they'd put the books into categories as they do with the non-fiction, that way I could pick out the thrillers more easily. David has occasionally picked out a 'Woman's' book for me by accident, a major disaster, I go mad if I haven't a good book I can really get into. I hate romance, yuck, and I can't read the same book twice.

Wednesday 9th ☆ I've realised today that I'm self-sufficient and what's more that I like it. I'm enjoying David's absence and, although thoughts of my treachery do threaten to overwhelm me, I'm managing to stem the flow.

I haven't cooked a dinner all week and the children are still alive. We've had fish fingers and crisps today – and cartons of yoghurt and orange juice to keep away beri-beri and the plague. We ate at half-past four because that's when we were hungry. I'd never realised before just how much David nags. I don't, at this moment, have a clue if his 'I'm a Tiger' T-shirt is in the ironing basket, airing cupboard, laundry basket, his drawer or the wardrobe and it doesn't matter a

damn. I am not required, for this brief week, to know. Neither am I being hauled off to bed when I'm in the middle of a tense, suspense-filled chapter simply because he's got designs on my person.

I'm lonely, but I'm always lonely and you can get used to anything. At least I'm free in my loneliness. I'm happy with suppers and bedtimes that I can choose and I don't miss televised football one little bit.

Lucy and Kate aren't noticeably pining either. Think I'll replace him with a cheque from Social Security.

Hope no one calls, I don't want anyone to disturb my sleepy dreamy lazy little world. There's only room for three.

Thursday 10th ☆ Well, Lilian's certainly left me with something to think about. She came late this morning with Edward in tow. I saw her car coming from the bedroom window, which gave me the vital edge. I was only half dressed, there were cornflakes and split milk all over the kitchen, toys everywhere. The ironing board was still up in the kitchen next to the ironing basket which was overflowing on to the floor. Lucy and Kate had dressed up in the clean washing and were plonked in front of the TV watching Playschool, filthy and draped in David's shirts, a pink bra and my knickers on their heads. Katie had weed on the floor. I groaned – a fairly mild reaction in the circumstances – and flew. Flung my clothes on as I raced downstairs, whipped the washing off the kids and shoved it and what was all over the floor into the basket, yelling at a startled Lucy and Kate as I went to go upstairs and put their bathers on. Swept the dishes into the sink, mopped up the milk and wee-wee and was shovelling toys into the cardboard carton – everything mixed up, lego bricks with doll's clothes etc – when she knocked at the front door. I was astounded at myself. If only I could keep that pace up all day. I plugged the iron in to give the impression I'd begun the ironing this morning instead of the day before yesterday, and went to and went to answer the door. She gave me a sickly grin and seemed nervous. I said, 'Hi, come on in,' and led her into the kitchen. She wasn't herself at all, I could sense a sad upset in her.

'Coffee?' I said brightly. Felt *I* was in control for once.

'Lovely, thanks very much.' She was unusually grateful.

Lucy and Kate came downstairs, Lucy more or less in her bikini and Kate naked with her costume in one hand. I told Lilian about her passion for nudity, trying to be funny to ease the atmosphere. She smiled weakly. I ushered the kids, including Edward, into the garden with half a pound of biscuits to keep them there and closed the back door. Lilian sat at the kitchen table, I made the coffee and sat down opposite her.

'Lovely day,' I said glancing through the window. I didn't know what to say. Lilian always controls our conversations.

'Mmm. It's my birthday.' She bit her bottom lip.

'Oh Lilian, I didn't know, I'd have sent you a card or something.'

'I'm forty-five Jane,' it snapped out. She examined my face for reaction. Her look flustered me. I turned red. 'Oh ... well, you don't look it.' *Wrong* thing to say.

'It's middle-aged isn't it? You regard it as middle-aged, don't you?'

It was difficult to gather my thoughts, to work out what to say, her words were so rapid and intent. 'Well ... it's no big deal Lilian. I don't think age is important, it's how you feel and think.'

'Mm. Well I've been thinking a lot lately and I feel old. Old and foolish.'

'Aw, come on Lilian, forty-five's not that old.' Second bloomer.

'Hm,' she turned sideways to me, gazing blankly through the upper part of the window. 'I've been planning a week-end away, you know just a quiet couple of days, me and Hugh on our own without the family.' She looked vaguely questioning, asking my approval, so I gave it.

'Hugh laughed at the idea!' She wanted me firmly on her side now.

'Why?' I said amazement in my voice. 'I think it's a great idea. He should be thrilled to bits you still want a week-end alone with him after all these years.'

'I thought it would be a bit like a second honeymoon,' she blurted it out with a pink face. 'I suppose it was a bit ridiculous, me and Hugh aren't the sort to have second honeymoons. I'd bought a new nightie as well, not *sexy* or anything' – the word was uncomfortable on her tongue. 'I got it in Marks, it's pretty, it was expensive.'

I've never seen Lilian so uncertain, so unsure of herself. It cost her a hell of a lot to come and talk about it. She must have been feeling really low. Hugh had told her he couldn't go on the week-end because he'd arranged to go fishing with Bob, his friend. Couldn't he cancel it. *Cancel fishing?* He couldn't disappoint Bob.

I thought she'd have been glad to have Nigel and Charles, her oldest children, home from college for the holidays but I was wrong.

'Jane,' she said matter of factly, straight from the shoulder, 'I've been dreading them coming. I've never admitted it before, not even to myself. They're selfish, they're lazy, the house will be full of their inconsiderate, untidy friends. They leave a stream of dirty dishes in the kitchen, dirty clothes all over their bedrooms, they treat me like a housekeeper.'

Lilian says she should have made a stand years ago, stood up for herself. She says it's a mistake to put them first all the time, you don't get any thanks for it. And she hasn't been feeling well, 'the change', and her legs ache a lot.

Friday 11th ☆ Took Lucy to the story-reading at the library today. Katie is officially too young, lower age limit is three and I can understand why. Considered lying about her age in my fight for freedom but it was unnecessary. She went over and sat beside Lucy, looking so cherubic and thrilled at the prospect of it all that the librarian let her stay. The mothers sat in the reference section, only place with chairs, like neurotic students suddenly excused the end of term exams. We couldn't chat, though, because we were in the library. Katie was as good as gold and she's been singing 'ten fat sausages' ever since. Will take them again next week, it's the final one. Lucy thinks the library is some kind of super-shop where you can get books without paying.

Bought them a Walt Disney lampshade in Woolworth's, assembled it and put it up and put a new light bulb in – and it works. Sounded like the Waltons tonight, 'Goodnight, Katie,' 'Goodnight, Lucy,' 'Goodnight, Mickey Mouse,' 'Goodnight, Donald Duck.' Mother's language is idiotic. The scorch mark where I dropped my fag on Pluto hardly shows now it's up.

Postcard from Cath today, Paul has joined them and they've all gone up to Scotland for a fortnight. Lucky beggars.

Saturday 12th ☆ David will be home tomorrow, so today was the day, as I said to the children, that we had to get their place sorted out, ready for the conquering hero's return. We've been rushing round like fools trying to make good the neglect of the past week. Impossible in twenty-four hours.

Bought David's favourite food in Johnson's superstores and thought I would use up the last of the bread-making ingredients in the form of hot cross buns. I was hotter and crosser than the buns, but they look good – like real ones.

Had hoped to greet David with a potful of Katie's four star and a great deal of motherly and daughterly pride, but no luck. Have tried especially hard this week, too.

I'd been looking forward to the film about the Cannes Film Festival on TV tonight but it was a bit of a let-down, the festival was tatty and silly. A group of American actors, publicising another epic western, boasting about their marvellous personal relationships by insulting one another with what was supposed to be wit. I think they only screened the programme to show the monumental knockers on display on the beach. Paul and Linda McCartney were on, the only good bit. They'll never know what they've done for me, their music's saved my sanity. If I'm feeling low a Wings LP will really lift me, if I'm feeling good it makes me feel better.

Sunday 13th ☆ David's back, a triumphal turn into the drive in our brand new company car, grin plastered all over his face, sunglasses on making him look sexy like he'd just got back from the Cannes Festival. We were all in the window watching for him in our best clothes and hairdos. He'd bought himself a new shirt, blue denim with lots of pockets, makes him look a smart long-distance lorry driver, I like a bit of rough, and he needed a shave. I walked my fingers up his chest and said, 'I like the shirt,' in my best Mae West. He said he knew I would that's why he wore it and he was ready to be ravished.

We enjoyed our special supper after the kids were in bed but I can't say that it was romantically intimate – it got better later – because he talked about his job all through it, wild with enthusiasm, never once asked how we'd managed. Said he was glad to be home, he's been staying in a two star hotel, beautiful place, he said, good food but he'd had to go into the bar every night, there was nothing else to do. God, the sheer deprivation.

Monday 14th ☆ The man does want the car, he'll bring the money up later in the week.

Got the washing done, it took ages as David brought rather a lot, like a suitcase-full, back with him.

Tuesday 15th ☆ Tidied upstairs, cleaned downstairs, tried to sort out the children's squabbles. Washed out urine-stained tiny pants, dried them, washed out more urine-stained tiny pants, dried them, washed out the first batch of re-urine-stained tiny pants. Decided to leave her naked. Didn't do the ironing, hate ironing in hot weather. Would like to get my hair cut if we sell the car but don't know where to go. It's a dicey business going to Hack the knife, Benton's answer to Vidal Sassoon.

Wednesday 16th ☆ Did the ironing, sewed buttons

on things. Always thought the point of nylon socks was that they didn't need darning. David's feet prove me wrong. Breast of lamb for tea which inflamed a full scale battle at tea-time. Lucy and Katie don't want cooked dinner in this weather, David faints off without. What can I do? Prepare different meals, I suppose, something I swore I'd *never* do after seeing friends tearing their hair out over sausages for one, chops for another etc. It's such a fag cooking a dinner and washing all those pans for one person. I never want a cooked meal either.

The man's been, paid for and taken away the car, felt quite sad to see it chug away. David's fixed a hairdressing appointment for me. Eleven on Saturday morning. Can't go to one of the good salons in Norwich really, it costs too much and the car money has to last.

Walked up to Lilian's but she was out. Went from there to Pauline's but she'd gone to her mother's, Cathy's still away. Came home and sat in the sun. Lucy and Katie were tired after the long walk. Felt lonely and cut off. Aeroplanes crawled across the sky glinting silver in the sun, the children and I gazed up at them wondering where they were going and where they'd come from. They could have been spacecraft from Mars. Hard to believe there's a world out there, high finance, business coups, people jetting from one continent to the next.

Friday 18th ☆ Not speaking to David, he's working tomorrow morning. He forgot all about my hair-dressing appointment, can't think of anything except the installation of new machines. They have to be ready before the men are taken on. 'Why?' I asked as if I didn't know the answer. He looked at me as if I was stupid, 'We'd lose production,' he said, as if that meant the world would end. I said he'd have to take Katie to work with him. I'd intended taking Lucy with me anyway, knew he couldn't cope with two of them. He told me not to be ridiculous. I said it was no more ridiculous than taking her to the hairdresser's with me. I'll have to call in and cancel while we're in Benton tomorrow. We'll have to go to the supermarket tomorrow afternoon because the Captain of British Industry was too tired to go tonight.

Saturday 19th ☆ I'm tamping mad, shaking with rage. Here I am captive in my own kitchen, my two little girls, *whose home this is*, are captive with me, separated from their toys which are in the living room. David's in there with Kenny and his horrible brother 'airy 'arry. They're swigging *my* tea and watching sport on the telly. We are barred because the girls are not mutes, they *dared* to speak at the same time as the sports commentator. I could have belted 'airy 'arry because it was he, not even their father, who looked impatient and said, 'Shush, keep quiet girls.' I was wild, who is he to tell *my* girls off, he's not fit to lick their boots. I flounced out, bringing Lucy and Kate with me. A bit later he poked his head round the living room door. 'Any chance of a cup of tea love?' he said, smiling, he thought he was charming, he thinks he's butch because he's got thick black hair on his arms, he always has his sleeves rolled up. I *glared*. 'Ooh, you're lovely when you're roused,' he said sliding his arm round my waist and pinching my side. I couldn't believe it, how dare he? I glared again, revolted, not charmed. 'Oh-oh,' he said, 'sorry I spoke.'

A bit later David came in and put the kettle on. He

114

didn't speak so I had to. 'You don't make coffee for them, it's too dear.'

'I was making tea.'

'They're lucky, aren't they?'

'Well you won't, will you?'

'No, I bloody well won't, forced out of my own living room, imprisoned in my own kitchen.'

'For God's sake, Jane, you don't *have* to sit in here, you can come back in there.'

'As long as I don't say a word and gag the girls. No thanks.'

'There's only this next race they want to watch. I'll get them out into the garage then.' He was conspiratorial and I knew he'd feel a ninny if he had to carry the tea into them, so I made it and took it in. I said 'Here you are, hope it chokes you', but with a smile so they'll never know for sure that I meant it. They'll have put me down as another hysterical female and think David has a lot to put up with. Women!

They're here because there's something wrong with Harry's van and they have a job on tomorrow, building a garden wall. It seemed to me that David was doing all the work, Kenny and Harry stood about watching whilst he wriggled and struggled underneath it and got oil on his clothes. I'll have to get the oil off. I have to go shopping. I've nothing to give the children for their tea but they can wait of course.

Sunday 20th ☆ Our heroine, me – and I choose the epithet with care, for anyone who changes Katie's overnight nappie is fully deserving of the title – is standing in the kitchen, knee deep in corn flakes, milk and lego bricks, clad in grubby dressing gown and slippers. Her hair stands out in frantic tufts or falls in lank loops over her face. It is half-past ten. She is fraught despite the hardworking drug chugging through her system in a valiumed attempt to calm the inner turmoil. The fruits of her womb hurtle around her feet, half naked and filthy, in joyful sabotage of all her bids for tidiness. The fruit of the egg of a geriatric hen lies rock hard, wrapped in icy polythene, in a pyrex dish. Our heroine is heard to shriek, 'Ah, stuff the bleedin' chicken,' and to suggest, with more than a hint of menace, that our hero, who lounges on the sofa with the colour supplement wondering where his life went wrong, takes his kids out. Half an hour passes and we find our heroine with two children, both of whom are ready to go out into the world, and one raw bird, euphemistically termed chicken, still rock hard and definitely not ready to go into the oven. Our heroine casts a sullen glance at the label on its scrawny white chest and ponders on the workings of the Trades Descriptions Act. Our hero, plus infants, passes through the back door, mentioning that dinner, or lunch, as he's just read the colour supplement, could be eaten at tea-time. Our heroine with the wild hair and terrible eyes screams that he should have given the Royal Assent before this so that she too could have gone for walkies. 'We'll wait for you,' he says with sweet reason. Naughty words issue from her sweet lips, the general meaning of which is 'get lost', because she is enraged at his reasonable tone. Then she changes her mind and commands he return until she has dressed. On second thoughts she instructs him to clear off. Hero and children move backwards and forwards like characters in a film with motion reversed to provide amusement.

As they depart our heroine burst into tears of remorse amongst the ruin that was once a kitchen and of despair that it is she who must effect the repair.

Monday 21st ☆ I leave my diary around, hoping that David will read it and understand me. I imagine the wonderfully close relationship that might follow. It's supposed to be secret, which would protect me from accusations of hurting, wounding or misunderstanding. But he never does read it, just as he's never read a letter addressed to me. I can't tell him all that's in my mind, he's not here enough, and as things flit through my mind I have to grasp hold of them, there and then. I can't wait until he gets home from work and the children are in bed. I don't think David rates thoughts and feelings. We're quite different in that way, he's practical, down to earth, I am not. He can't even remember the golden eagle he saw on honeymoon in Scotland. I remember not only the eagle but the tree, the road, the exact spot where we saw it. It's a treasured memory and I often think of it, the bird circling above the leafless tree. We can't share that. All my life I've wished for someone to share my thoughts with. I used to think that someone would be David.

I just wish he so *desperately* wanted to know me that he'd do something drastic like reading my private diary.

Pauline and the kids came this morning at half-past nine, which isn't the best time to visit me, especially in the school holidays. She was cheesed off, really cheesed off, couldn't bring herself to face the washing and the same old routine, did I ever feel like it? I was amazed at how much I've obviously concealed from her. I said it would be easier to list the times when I didn't feel like that. Then she got on to her relationship with Kenny, which is the root of her depression. They argue all the time about her job. She's ready to confess that she enjoys it but he won't agree that it's also necessary if they're to do more than barely exist. It's his nights out

117

which are cut down by her working evenings – that's what it is. He wants her to be a happy little woman, content to cook food and raise children – and leave him alone. She can't be that. 'There's got to be more,' she said, 'There's got to be more than this.' She's tried to talk to him about it but it's no good. She wants to save up for a house of their own, she thinks if they really got stuck in, Kenny and Harry could make out better than they are doing. Kenny won't listen. He's on the sick, his back he says. She compared him with David, 'David's out there grafting for you and the kids,' she said, 'you'll be doing the house up, you've got a new car, you'll be having a phone in. If only Kenny'd pull with me instead of against me all the time.'

I thought she'd have felt better after blasting off but she didn't seem a lot happier when she left. I don't know what to think, it seems to me that Kenny just doesn't love her, has no feeling for her at all, she says they never make love and there is no marriage without sex. Pauline must feel something for Kenny or she wouldn't work so hard at their marriage. Perhaps she would. Maybe she has nothing else.

Tuesday 22nd ☆ Am beginning to have doubts about my rash invitation to Diana and Nick. It's not that I don't want to see them, I do, I'm looking forward to it. It's the house. I'm going to have to clean it. I should never have conjured up that sun-dappled, stripped pine kitchen image, earthenware jugs stuffed with buttercups and daisies and so on. But I didn't think they'd ever come and the fantasy did me good. What if she opens the oven door and reveals the secrets of my unclean cooker? Who knows what may be growing under the bed? Can't rely on David for practical help or even moral support, he's too busy having tiny anxiety crises all over the place, that is when he isn't suffering delusions of grandeur about what tomorrow will bring. They're interviewing applicants for jobs at the new factory. I *do* hope all goes well for him but I'd hope that without all this drama. Have pressed his suit, shirt, tie. but draw the line at cleaning his shoes. I don't get angry any more at performing the duties of a valet, it's a much more serious emotion. I despise him for being so feeble. A fully grown adult male who considers himself able to manage the production in a factory should be able to cope with pressing his own clothes.

Feel lonely and completely out of touch with the world, school holidayitis.

Thursday 24th ☆ I've cleaned the house today in its entirety, cause for celebration. It's so awful cleaning for people who are going to stay, never know where they'll wander and what if they drop a hairgrip behind the dressing table? Or open the fridge and see the congealed blood left from last week's liver? I whizzed through it all today with a light heart and it doesn't matter if Diana does drop a hairgrip behind the dressing table or open the fridge door because everything is clean. If the kids do anything destructive, like playing, before Saturday I'll ... I'll ... have to do it all over again.

David hasn't painted the staircase wall or filled in the holes in the dining room. He says you can't start decorating just because you have visitors coming, they'll have to take us as they find us. Mucky. Great. He's really on top of the world, they took on men for the works and women for the office and they all start work on Tuesday.

Don't know what I'm going to give Diana and Nick to eat. They're bound to be used to lasagne and quiche, I'll bet they know what creme brulée is. Hope they find sausage and mash a quaint novelty. Feel I should be able to toss a salad now that I'm married to an executive, well sort of.

Friday 25th ✩ What a hectic day, shopping in Benton this morning and supermarket this evening. I'm not used to all this activity, but we're all much too happy to feel tired, David gets his enormous new salary cheque next week, the car money, what's left of it, in the bank, they've ordered a phone for us, Diana and Nick are coming tomorrow and most of the work is done, my cup runneth over.

Had hoped to leave Katie at the story-reading today to sneak away for a beautifully solitary look at the shops but her ladyship, independent little creature of last week, looked ready to howl if I so much as picked up my bag and headed for the reference section today, so the librarian said that I could sit in on the story. What could I do? The only mother picked out for such high honour. I sat on the floor with the under fives, all agog for Leo the Lion who bloomed.

Saturday 26th ✩ They're here, say I in tones of hushed awe. Diana's Joy de Patou stands beside the Boots Family Talc on the bathroom windowsill. They're sleeping in our bed, between our best wedding present, blue flowery sheets which are worn dangerously thin in parts but as long as they don't do anything too energetic they should make it through two nights. Not sure that D and I measure up to having friends like Diana and Nick any more but it's flattering to think that we do and the brand new Scimitar GTE parked outside doesn't hurt the old ego. I'm glad David's got his Cortina; though lowly by comparison, it is new. The car and his new job give a boost to his masculine pride, which I think's suffered in recent years. He can keep his end up now.

Diana and Nick are so fit and energetic. They've no children. David and I look in desperate need of vitamins by comparison. They're both tanned, the Seychelles last month and the Canaries last February – they go cheap in the winter. Diana looks wonderful. She was wearing denims, the sort that fit like a second skin and a T-shirt that had obviously been bought abroad and not at an overseas branch of Marks and Spencer's. Her hair is chin length, a coppery dark brown, falling immaculate and gleaming from a centre parting. As their car drew up outside she was leaning from the passenger window with large sunglasses pushed up on to her head, and looked like a film star.

Nick hasn't changed at all, still thin, vital as if he's supercharged. He wore denims too and a fine cream sweater. I used to wear a lot of cream. They talked to the children, both of whom were swept away by the glamour of it all. Diana followed me into the kitchen and examined the kids' paintings hanging on the doors with genuine interest. Imagine someone taking an interest. It's wonderful. And the benefits of conversation cannot be overstressed, wish you could get it on the national health instead of Valium. I have to rely on visits from Diana and the Michael Parkinson show. Diana and Nick asked me about the joys and otherwise of being a full-time wife and mother, they really wanted to know, no one's ever asked me before. I gave a poor account of myself, can't express myself any more. Their questions were answered by my embarrassment as I struggled to find the right words. I could see in their eyes that they were worried at my appearance. Not seeing me often, they notice a change. They said they've almost decided not to have any children.

They want to look round the village tomorrow, hope they're not expecting it to be quaint and studded with craftsmen and writers of thrillers. It's wonderful to have them here, I feel excited. I suppose I'm reminded of when I felt fit and energetic and good-looking too.

Sunday 27th ☆ Been out for a drink, the Three Feathers, couldn't take D and N to the Crown except to flaunt them. Felt strange being in a pub. Didn't tell anyone, they'd have thought me a real hick, but didn't know what to order. Felt I'd never been in a pub before, kept looking round, drinking it all in, the fashions, the behaviour, some of the drinkers looked so young. I'm out of touch with grown-up pleasures, tonight made me realise how important they are. I must somehow manage to include them in my life.

I thought Diana looked stunning tonight, but when we got to the pub she only looked the same as everyone else. It was me that looked dowdy. Everyone in the pub was glamorous; healthy glows, gleaming skins and hair. I wore my matronly dress which I still haven't paid for.

D and N have reminded me how David and I used to be. He doesn't know what I'm on about as usual, he thinks everything in the garden's lovely and we're the same as D and N because of his new status. 'And *we've* got two kids,' he said. Maybe David *is* the same. The money and everything will make a difference but there's a lot more to it than that, it's the state of mind.

It's one's state of mind, self-confidence that puts glows on cheeks and sparkles in eyes. I used to be sharp, I used to feel attractive, I used to feel part of things when I had a job. I didn't notice the gaps between David and me because I could fill them with other people, other things. Now I have to depend so much on him for companionship and entertainment, I wonder if our relationship can stand up to it. I wonder if how I feel at the moment isn't the feeling behind many divorces.

I keep thinking of Cathy and her 'O' level. Maybe I should take a leaf out of her book, think of going back to work. A new career, train for something I *really* want to do. But I know it's impossible with the children and living so far from Norwich and training facilities. Could there be a way round the huge practical difficulties? There would be if we lived at home, my mother, and maybe if we lived at home just seeing Diana and Nick would cure my depression. Here I only meet housewives who presumably all feel as flattened as I do. I feel I've been squashed and subdued over the last few years until there's not much of what was once me left. I hate taking Valium but it's worse when I don't. I have to be totally submerged, there's no time or space for 'me'. Me is divided up into three, and it feels at the moment as if the cutting up has killed it. It caters to David and Lucy and Kate. It's too busy being supporting, encouraging, reassuring to keep its own life going, it has no time and less opportunity.

Monday 28th ☆ Been to Magna Martyr for a picnic. Magna Martyr is a fantastic place, fantastic in the real sense of the word. We turned off the dual carriageway on to a winding country lane. There are thatched cottages with piles of logs outside and hollyhocks in the gardens. It was like going through a time warp, didn't see a soul, which added to the mystery of it all. We parked the car by a derelict farm cottage. There were plum trees in the wild tangle that was once its garden, absolutely dripping with fruit. I've brought a fruit laden bough home, I like to look at it. We walked the rest of the way. It was too hot to keep the kids cooped up in the car. We saw strange fungi that I've never seen before growing on the dead stumps of trees, and there were sand lizards. I've never seen them before either. At the bottom of the road was an incredible mountain of sand and beside it the ruins of a monastery. My imagination ran riot and I twittered on about times past, touching the old stones, expecting sensation, and looked amongst the rubble for signs of ancient bloodshed. All I found were signs of the ice cream van hidden round the corner with stacks of parked cars and *people*. So much for my supernatural glade. They all laughed and David said I hadn't been the same since I read *The Bloxham Tapes*.

We had our picnic at the foot of the sand mountain with the other families. We found a place and sat down to watch the floorshow. Two couples, the men slim and fit, the women flabby and thickened by childbirth stepped out to play ball. Their children sat on the sidelines, forbidden to join in and looking glumly on as their parents made fools of themselves. Everyone sitting there was riveted, though they pretended not to be. The two women had 'Olympia Health Club' emblazoned across their T-shirts, their breasts bounced and bumped about as they ran and leapt for the ball. One of the men tackled one of the women, bringing her down. A lot of laughter and giggling, false on her part, she was horribly embarrassed. So were their children.

Diana and Nick have gone now, I'm miserable, I love them, their visit has done me so much good. No preparations for their journey home, they just put everything back in their holdall. I suppose without nappy changes and potty stops on the hard shoulder and crumpled sandwiches the journey doesn't seem so long.

We waved them off, shouting repeat invitations, the kids saying please, David and I begging. It's been heavenly, time out, but very expensive in food, good job we've got the car money.

Tuesday 29th ☆ She's done it. Katie's done it. Scored a direct hit on her potty. I'm so proud of her. I knew it was impending. She always stands still and looks blank faced in an expectant sort of way. Mummies are expert in judging these important little moments. I whipped her pants down, pushed her on to the pot and snarled menacingly, 'Shit you little bugger' and she did. I think she was scared. We hugged each other and danced round the room in delighted accomplishment. 'I sick in pot,' she said with a grin and shining eyes. 'No, love,' I began, 'not sick sh ...' What's a word at a time like this? There's poetry in motion.

September

Friday 1st ☆ Happy birthday Dad. Another hot day, felt lazy, in a warm dull stupor. Bored out of my lonely mind? Played pouring water in the pool with Lucy and Kate. Made more funnels and fountains out of empty washing-up liquid bottles. Katie said, 'Cor! Thanks mum!'

Supermarket this evening. Have extended my one-woman boycott of goods with offensive TV commercials to beef stock cubes.

Leighton called – without his woolly hat! He has a shock of black curly hair. He was transformed.

Monday 4th ☆ Back to school today. Everyone at the school gates looked half-dead. Cathy looked pale and tired though still very pleased with her grade B 'O' level pass. Pauline looked drawn and fed-up to the teeth, and even Lilian looked woebegone. Janice said, 'All this work in the house is really getting me down, Jane.' I said 'Haven't they finished *yet?*' 'No,' she said, 'they're putting central heating in as well now. My husband's friend only comes when he feels like it and what can you say, he's doing us a favour.' However does she manage?

I watched Cathy walk away from the school towards the shop. She walked like an old woman, tired and aching, pushing the pushchair with one hand, had her shopping basket in the other and one eye on Lyndsey and Gareth as they ran up steps and dodged in doorways dangerously near the road. There was a time when the sight of her would have meant nothing to me, just a pregnant woman with her children, but now I know how it feels, the aches, the heaviness, the anxiety and tension.

Lilian gave me another pile of magazines today, like the home improvement ones. She says she's still feeling under the weather.

David's new boss is moving into his house in Benton on Saturday. David had promised to go and help.

There's a notice in the Post Office about night school classes in Benton, enrolment next week. Will look into it, maybe I can move musically or throw pots to stimulate my mind.

Friday 8th ☆ Pauline came this afternoon, she's very low. Kenny has gone back to work with his brother. He still refuses to help around the house or be involved in any way. She said she doesn't want help any more, she wants him to share the responsibility now. If he'd even tried to understand why she needed to escape from the house, if he'd give a hand, if only occasionally, her attitudes would never have hardened as they have now. She doesn't see why he can't get the girls ready for bed, he's home by five, she catches the twenty-past five bus. She doesn't see why the week-end chores can't be split down the middle, she doesn't see why he can't learn what there is to be done and how to do it without being asked. She did. 'If the potatoes are boiling over in front of his eyes he doesn't even know how to turn the gas down, and he doesn't want me,' she said, and described as 'pathetic' her attempts to make him want her. 'I dab perfume on and brush my hair and wear my blue nightie and ... oh ... all sorts of things. I must be daft. If he cared anything for me he'd want me, wouldn't he? I know I'm not Raquel Welch, but it'd be normal to want me, wouldn't it? I wish he'd go, I don't know why he stays. He doesn't want me or the kids.'

I felt a failure, I didn't know what to say.

I told her about my boycott of things in the supermarket to try and make her laugh. Seemed silly – it is. She added a perfume to the list but it didn't give us much satisfaction as neither of us would have bought it anyway.

Saturday 9th ☆ David didn't get in till half-past eleven, been helping his new boss and family move into their new house. He raved about the house, told me I'd love it. I raved for different reasons. He said what could he have done. Brad, the boss, had wanted to buy him a drink for helping. I said I'd helped by looking after his children so that he was free to go. He looked at me mystified. He saw Kenny with the strange girl again, he's fairly sure it's the same girl he saw him with before. There are times when I feel close to murdering some people.

Sunday 10th ☆ Offered hot cross buns with afternoon tea. 'It's a shame,' said David, tossing one up and down in his hand like a cricket ball. 'We can't even feed them to the birds, they'd never get off the ground with a lump of this inside them.'

Monday 11th ☆ Can't go to night school in Benton, David phoned about the classes today, although I'm prepared to do absolutely anything. All the classes start at seven, that would mean catching the ten to six bus and David's not home in time for me to do that. In any case I'd have to walk about a mile to the college from the bus stop in Benton and I don't fancy that on cold winter nights, not even for first year cookery.

Asked David to talk to me tonight. He said 'What about?' I said anything apart from gossip and pregnancy and keeping house. We had nothing to say to each other. Our worlds are miles apart. He's involved with his job, I'm involved with the children and by eight o'clock, when we're usually sitting together and childless, we're too tired to make the effort

Thursday 14th ☆ Cathy says it's known in the village about Kenny and his girl. The girl's name is Jeannette, she's an old flame, she and Kenny were courting when he met and married Pauline. Cathy's giving education a rest until next year but she's not giving up her long term ambitions.

Monday 18th ☆ Been leafing through the mags Lilian gave me, load of rubbish, choice between what Diana Dors thinks about show business marriages, a chance to win Bill Maynard's bedroom and a riveting article entitled 'Boobs, Bottoms and Bulging Tums'.

According to the magazines, there is no reason why I should be bored. Not when I could do any of the following; paint a picture, make a model boat, mend a puncture, milk a goat, brew wine from nettles, sew a patchwork, sail a boat, make bread, fly a plane, ford a river, make an effort. Every day is an effort I have to make.

Tuesday 19th ☆ Lovely day today. Took advantage of the sun – already tried the milkman but Leighton isn't such a heavenly body. Did the washing. Washing machine definitely in trouble now, puddles all over the kitchen floor. Like mopping up after the great flood. Took the children to Alcatraz after school. Never really believed in the existence of those interesting snatches of conversation that writers are supposed to overhear and build whole stories around until today. Three women in a huddle at the playground; one said, 'Well, if you're having it off you're having it off and that's all there is to it.'

Hugh called in this evening. David had arranged to do the engine on the new car, petrol consumption. He came in for a cup of coffee but wouldn't stay long, he was very concerned about Lilian. He says she has a very bad leg and is running a temperature. He's having a day off work tomorrow to take her to the doctor's. She should have gone long before this.

Thursday 21st ☆ I've won sixty pounds tonight, never won anything before. Tonight was the night that Cathy and I had our initiation into the El Dorado Bingo Club. I was Ethel Webster and Cath was Charlotte Shite, we *couldn't* stop laughing. Did Charlotte Shite in the sugar or was it Charlotte that shat on the cat. Those were the names on the membership cards that Pauline had got hold of to get us in. We didn't want to go to the extreme of joining. It's been one of those silly, giggly nights. The grandfatherly old man sitting in front of Cathy told her he'd had a virgin last week – he meant none of the numbers on his card had been called. The woman behind me complained disgustedly about her cards. 'All the ones on this one, look, 31 61, 71, and *this* card

has 90 and 1 together.' She looked at me, waiting for outraged sympathy. '*Oh*, how *awful* for you,' I said. I peeked at Cathy's card, all the ones, no chance, smug smirk, I had talked with an expert.

We had to settle down quietly when play began, like the start of a lesson at school, but no one fidgets at Bingo or whispers to their friends, everyone was very intent and silent. The high spot of the evening was the 'Big Link' with King's Lynn. A disembodied voice came through the loudspeaker, 'Hello to you, the El Dorado in *Benton*!'. 'Hello, King's Lynn' shouted our announcer and then we all had to shout 'Hello, King's Lynn.' The woman behind me said they do this at holiday camps too, they link you up with other holiday camps. '*Great*,' she said with nodding head and narrowed eyes. Cathy and I giggled secretly. 'Hey shut-up,' I said, 'this is the *Big Link*.' You could sense the tension, everybody in King's Lynn and Benton competing for four hundred pounds. I was surprised at so much prize money. Cathy dropped her card and got a bit flustered. A few numbers later she called 'here' in a thin reedy embarrassed voice, she looked down at her card again and slowly up at the numbers called which were displayed on the stage, and then she looked horrified. But it was too late. Pauline was the the end of the row checking her card, the woman beside Cath had snatched it from her and passed it along the row. 'You've called *wrong*,' whispered Pauline as if she'd known we'd do something to let her down.' 'sa bogey, 'sa bogey,' rippled round the hall. We gathered it was a pretty serious offence at any time but in the *Big Link* ...! Our announcer was covered in confusion and embarrassment as he had to apologise to our friends in King's Lynn. A bit later on I really did win a house and all the old ladies with dyed black hair and flashing gems turned round to look, ' 'sthem that called a bogey,' they said with knowing nods, ' 'sthem that called a bogey.'

We've shared it, twenty pounds each. We had a bag of chips and a good laugh waiting for the bus home. Pauline says we embarrassed her and we haven't to go again until we know what to do. And he's *not* an announcer for Chrissakes, he's a *caller*. It's far too complicated for me to grasp the finer points.

Saturday 23rd ☆ Lilian is dead. I can't bear to write it, and I can't believe it even though I have. While I was grumbling at the crowds in the supermarket, while I was complaining of being tired standing in the queue, Lilian died. It doesn't seem right. I should have known, should have felt, but I didn't. We drove home, David was irritated by other drivers, I shouted at the girls to sit still and keep quiet and all the time Lilian was dying. Mrs J came to tell me today. She made us both a cup of tea and told me that Lilian had died of a clot of blood on the lungs, and, she'd been told, Lilian would be alive now if she'd sought medical help earlier. It's a very rare occurence.

I keep thinking of the saying 'In the midst of life there is death'. It's trite but very true. I just can't believe it.

Monday 25th ☆ Am still stunned by Lilian's death. We all are.

Tuesday 26th ☆ Lilian's funeral is on Friday. David's going, we've sent flowers. The village just won't be the same without her. Everyone knew her, she was so involved with everything.

Cathy staggered down today. We've been talking about our futures, what we'll do when the kids are all in school. It was nice to dream. That's all it was, dreaming, though Cathy would disagree. There'll always be school holidays and hours before school starts and hours after school ends.

Wednesday 27th ☆ Been to Pauline's tonight and I'm still not sure if I should have. For one thing she should have been working but I'd forgotten, I'm still not thinking straight after the shock of Lilian's death. Pauline was at home because she'd worked a night last week for Betty, who was sick, and Betty had turned up tonight to work for Pauline who had hurried home to her husband which is what started all the trouble. Kenny had left by the time I got there, which is just as well as I couldn't have looked him straight in the eye and may have done grievous bodily harm after what I saw tonight. Brave words. I don't know what I'll do when I next meet Kenny, I don't know what I'm supposed to do in these situations. I had a shock when Pauline opened the door, both her cheeks were bright red, her right eye was swelling and there was a cut on her cheekbone. His ring did that. She'd obviously been crying but she said she was glad to see me, she wanted someone to talk to. My first thought was that she'd found out about Jeannette, but it wasn't that. Suddenly let off work, she'd raced to the fish and chip shop, thinking fish and chips for supper and her presence would set the right kind of scene for herself and Kenny to have a civilised talk about things. But it didn't. When she got home she found she'd forgotten her key so she had to knock. Her neighbour's son had answered the door. Kenny had been upstairs getting ready to go out. It seems Tony from next door has

134

been founding a baby-sitting empire for himself on all the nights that Pauline works. She was livid, furious. 'All his talk about *me* never being here, when is *he* here? Look at this, kid.' Embarrassedly she rolled up her sleeve and showed me an enormous bruise on her upper arm where he'd punched her. 'You can see what sort of a family we are.' She was ashamed. 'Come and look in here,' she beckoned me into the kitchen, 'this is where it all happened.'

God, what a mess. There were bits of fish and chip everywhere, greasy newspapers screwed up and chucked about the floor, a vinegar bottle spilling half its contents had rolled under the sink – a shambles. 'He threw them at me,' she said.

'Looks like you threw them back.'

'That's when he hit me.'

We cleared up the mess. It must have been one helluva row. We sat on the living room carpet with our mugs of tea. I felt like the worst kind of hypocrite sitting there, listening to her pouring her heart out, knowing, as I did, about Kenny seeing another woman on top of all his other crimes. I said, 'What are you going to do Pauline?'

'I don't know,' she sighed deeply, 'I've got three children upstairs. I can't support them on my wages from the Bingo hall.'

It made me hurt to look at her battered face, she looked so different. I'm deeply shocked. I've never known anything like this before. I've persuaded Pauline to come to the market with Cathy and me tomorrow, to spend her Bingo winnings. She said she didn't feel like it, I said it would do her good so in the end she agreed.

Friday 29th ☆ Lilian's funeral today. I walked down

135

to watch them leave the house, pressing myself back against the wall of the house across the road, I didn't want to be noticed. Katie, in the pushchair, watched silently, absorbed with her packet of sweets. David didn't see us. I tried not to associate the coffin with my visual memories of Lilian. I cried today, the first time, I've been too numb with shock. Edward was there. He's such a little boy, only ten.

October

Tuesday 3rd ☆ Bought a shirt for David's birthday on the market today. It's brown and white checks, he's been fancying one for ages and he's short of clothes. I'm pleased with it. I bought wallpaper for the girls' bedroom too, really pretty, sprigs of tiny flowers on a white background. Hope to persuade David to part with some car money for matching curtain material. Pauline bought a continental quilt cover, a lamp shade, two treasure chests full of toys for the girls and lots of clothes for Scott. She said she felt like Viv Nicholson the pools winner, Spend Spend Spend. She was embarrassed at meeting Cathy today. Fortunately I got there first to explain, which proves I'm not always late. Pauline had camouflaged her bruises as well as she could. I winced to see her smile. We didn't talk about it, she's not ready yet, still thinking.

Cathy saved her money. It went into her fund for a new dining room suite. She left us at the market, it was her day for clinic at the hospital. I brought Gareth and Lyndsey home here after school. Cathy got back around half-past five. She was exhausted, Damian had been crotchety all afternoon and she's had to stand again at the clinic, you'd think they'd have got enough chairs by now, it was just the same when Pauline and I were going. It's no fun standing up for two hours when you're eight months pregnant. She had to wait for half an hour in a gown that'd been worn by two hundred mothers before her and had a split at the back, neck to hem, and no means of fastening. She said there were a lot of husbands there today too and some men cleaning the windows. It's bad enough exposing all and your bottle of wee-wee to the staff let alone the general public. I was reminded of Chris, a friend at home, and her adventure in her gown with the split up the back. When her labour pains started she was so frightened she climbed out of the ward window and ran off into the rhododendron bushes. The porters went in pursuit and the one who caught her told her it was the sight of her round pink bum had given her away.

Sunday 8th ☆ The winter is awful.

David says its common knowledge up the Crown about Kenny and his girl. He's surprisingly dis-approving. Disapproval I would expect from him but I'm surprised at the degree. Talking about it made me realise that I take David's faithfulness for granted. It never enters my head that he might fancy someone else, so I asked him tonight if he ever had. At first he said no but I kept on at him until he admitted that he liked to look but that was as far as it would ever go. 'Like me,' I said. That shocked him. He wanted to know who I looked at, but I couldn't think of anyone off hand so I said darkly 'Never you mind.' He said he's enough of a man to keep me happy, so I said I expect him to prove it, so he said he would, so I'm going to bed now.

Thursday 12th ☆ The quilt cover that Pauline bought on the market turned out to be a double sheet, the lamp shade won't fit her lamp, the girls' treasure chests contained only five toys apiece – not the advertised seven, Scott's clothes are OK but she hasn't washed them yet.

The man come to repair the TV. I confessed that it might have been Katie, David told me not to. He was very nice about it, but I had bribed him with a fag and a cup of tea.

I may, say I, drunk with power, add a brand of beefburgers to my boycott.

Lucy's harvest festival next week.

Sunday 15th ☆ How is it that a frail and feminine person like me can wallpaper most of a room successfully, unaided but hindered by two infants who want to help, and yet a skilled man like David needs a labourer – me – to put up the last four drops?

Hate rainy Sundays. Wonder what Diana and Nick do on Sundays? People visit their mothers on Sundays, or their mothers visit them. I wish my family could visit me, that would be wonderful. I'd make cakes and clean the house, put flowers in the living room, it would seem worth it. I wonder if Mrs J and Ernest would come next week? They might think me silly, asking neighbours to tea, but they'd be a kind of substitute grandma and grandad. It might feel like a family gathering.

Tuesday 17th ☆ Lucy's harvest festival in school. She sang her little heart out, mine burst with pride. She'd been selected to recite a poem and had kept it secret from me so that I'd have 'a lovely surprise, Mum'. Keeping it a secret for so long at five years old, and all to please me. I cried, gave myself a headache, felt quite somebody among the other mothers. Hope she never does play at Wimbledon, don't think I could stand it. Edward was in the choir, Hugh and his mother came to see him sing. Broke my heart to see them.

Thursday 19th ☆ Programme on TV last night about people, women in particular, taking drugs. David said I'd better watch. I really didn't want to, I don't need a television documentary to tell me it's not good to take drugs, I already know that. There was an American TV producer on the programme who'd become dependent on Valium after believing, as I did, that it was impossible. But the way I see it is either I take Valium, risk addiction but feel calmer, more capable and able to eat, or I don't take Valium, risk depression and starvation and become a nervous, miserable wreck. I don't think I have any choice at least until Katie is in school. I expect I'll feel more relaxed with more time to myself. I was planning on getting a job then, but I think I'm going to need at least twelve months off to recover from the past six years, or eight years it will be by then.

The TV repair man came back today. He was glad to come, had a hangover and asked if I minded if he sat down for ten minutes. Gave him tea and aspirin, he looked better when he left, so did the picture on the TV.

Leighton's branched out into yoghurt!

Mrs J and Ernest can't come to tea on Sunday because Geoff and Carla are coming for a long weekend.

Sunday 22nd ☆ I'm thinking of a sex change operation. I can see that David and I are going to live to be at least a hundred which gives me another

141

seventy years to master the art of housekeeping. When I get to the pearly gates, what's the betting St Peter's robe needs a wash. I feel like a Roman Catholic nurse assigned life-long duties on the abortion ward.

Going home for half-term next week – yippee.

Thursday 26th ☆ We're going home for a week tomorrow and Cathy hasn't produced. It's bound to happen while we're away, everything always does. I went up to see her this afternoon. She looked on edge, only able to control her nerves because I was there. 'Yes,' she agreed, 'I am edgy but it's only because the kids are home from school, I'm OK really and I'm *not* depressed. I think it's because everything's inevitable now. No point worrying about this baby any more, it's here alive and kicking' – she put a hand on her bump and the baby gave an enormous kick as if on cue. We laughed. 'There's no point getting in a sweat about 'O' and 'A' levels. I often wondered if I wasn't making life unnecessarily hard you know, doing all that, because it's just not on, it's out of the question. I'm sad about it, I did really want to go on with it, but I will, another twelve months or so and I'll start again. And once I get the birth over with' – she pulled a face – 'I'll have two days in hospital with nothing to see to except the baby, my meals brought to me, I can lie back and be a vegetable. I'll have Paul and my mother here to help when I come out.'

All the time we were talking the children, off school with colds, were in and out, they had felt-tipped pens but wanted to paint, could they have jars of water, could they keep the jars for ever, 'Mum, I *need* it for my pencils,' 'Gareth can't have that one, I want it.' Damian, the baby is into everything, Paul's records, newspapers that his father hasn't read yet. Cathy gave in to everything, hoping the older ones would leave us in peace, nervously watching the children's feet as they just missed the coffee cups on the floor, keeping an eye on the felt pens as the children put their colouring books on the settee and the carpet. Great jubilation, she's finally saved enough for her dining room suite.

Sunday 29th ☆ I can't stand it, here I am at home and I can't stand it. We've been out visiting, we have to, my mother insists, tinned salmon tea with elderly relatives. I can't stand the calm quiet orderliness of it all. They're never cross or miserable or wildly happy. I want to jerk them out of placid quietness, pass a note round with 'smile if you had it last night' written on it. I wouldn't dare, not in that sedate gathering of watch chains and crimplene dresses. But they'd somehow make it seem nothing – after the initial shock. They'd put it down to strain or something and never speak of it again.

I asked my mother tonight if she ever feels like a servant. I said she never sits down and enjoys our company, she just does things for us. Her good, kind, loving face looked startled and a bit upset. She made quiet, inarticulate sounds. I forced her to think about it. She didn't want to. I wanted to know. 'Didn't you ever want a job, Mum? I don't mean in the mill. Didn't you ever want the kind of job you wanted for me and Simon? Didn't you ever feel fed up just being a married woman?' I shocked her; mild words by my standards but enough to shock my mother.

'I'm not educated Jane, I haven't had schooling like you and Simon.' I wanted to yell that I hadn't had great schooling either but a couple of 'O' levels and being chief clerk at White Rose Engineering is the height of academic success to my mother, for a girl, and I kept quiet so she'd go on. 'We didn't have the opportunities in my day that you have.' I'm sick of hearing it. I'll never say that to Lucy and Kate, though I expect it will be just as true when they grow up.

'Your father's health hasn't been good for a long number of years now, Jane, and I had your gran to look after.' She thought I was getting at her. It hurt me because I wasn't, I wish I could *be* like her. It would make life a lot simpler. Then David and my father came back from the pub so the subject was dropped.

Tuesday 31st ☆ They were talking this afternoon, David and his father and brothers, as if they thought nuclear war was bound to happen. Stuart, the youngest, said 'It's not a question of if, it's a question of when, where and which side presses the button.' He was quite matter of fact about. It terrifies me. 'Ay, tek na notice,' said mother-in-law coming out of the kitchen, rolling her sleeves up to clear the decks for action, moving the junk from the table so she could set it for tea. ' 'e wunt tork like that if 'e'd lived through last 'un. Tek na notice love, if it 'appens it 'appens an' if it dunt it dunt. Tha's nowt we can do about it.'

She's right but I still think I'll ask Father Christmas for a fallout shelter. I'm frightened.

November

Wednesday 1st ☆ David's birthday and Sara's, we've all been on for tea. David loved his shirt, he looked across at me with a truly loving look when he opened the package and we smiled at each other – across the crowded room, some enchanted evening. When we're out and away from the house he becomes a man then, not just the husband who leaves hair in the sink and smokes in the bedroom. I see him as a stranger, a dishy stranger.

Sara was annoyed with me. She told me off which upset me, a) because she had right on her side and b) because I'm very fond of her, she's more like a sister than a sister-in-law. She asked me what had happened to the bush she'd given me. Without thinking I blurted out, 'Oh, *that* one. Lucy and Kate trampled it to death.' She was furious, 'I spent weeks cultivating that bush for you, it would have been lovely in your back garden. That's why I gave it to you. I would have liked it for myself, you know. I thought you were into gardening, I wouldn't have given it to you otherwise.' The others wandered back into the kitchen then, so we had to shut up; my mother gets upset if she thinks any of us have fallen out. I whispered 'sorry' and looked abject. I felt terrible but things improved after I'd broken the plate. Mum and I were washing up, Sara had taken the rubbish out to the bin, and just as she stepped back into the kitchen I dropped a tea plate. It was willow pattern, she collects it. 'Oh, Jane,' she said, 'never mind, it was cracked,' philosophical now, and then with a smile, 'I get the cracked ones out when you're coming, like to make things easy for you.'

I didn't eat my potatoes at lunchtime. I didn't want them, I looked at them and thought about being thirty and didn't eat them. My mother said 'You haven't eaten your potatoes Jane.' I said 'No, I haven't.' It was easy.

Thursday 2nd ✩ Tonight has been wonderful. I've felt like a character in a novel by Howard Spring, one of those about working-class youths who grow up to become leading policitians in the Lábour Party and have stacks of interesting conversations on the way. We went to Diana's but they were out, we tracked them down to Nick's mother's house and were invited in to join the party. There was Diana and Nick, Nick's brother and his wife, Nick's parents and of course David and I. It began with everyone admiring our new car and went on to David's new job and Nick's brother warning David not to forget his shop floor origins now that he was management. The conversation got on to politics and governments, we talked about everything, and everyone, including the women, said what they thought. It was great. No one thought about giving or taking offence, however heated the battle. We had wine and whisky and beer and ham sandwiches and we talked until one in the morning.

Nick's parents live in a dreary street. They look out on to a facing terrace at the front and factories at the back and I loved it. It was raining lightly when we left, the road shiny with wetness. I looked down the street at the neat row of soot-blackened houses, no front gardens, no trees to soften the hard walls and paving stones. Immaculately white net curtains and carefully applied paint. I felt the rain on my face and happy and at home.

Sunday 5th ✰ Got back last night, uneventful but much more comfortable journey down. Feel sad, heavy heart and homesick.

The Grans had bought fireworks for the kids so we had a bit of a bonfire in the back garden. We raked up a pile of leaves, there was a great drift of them beside the hedge. I enjoyed it but I did so wish we had someone to share it with – my family, really. I went to see if Mrs J and Ernest would come round but they were out.

Haven't seen anyone since we've been back, longing to know how Cathy is.

Thursday 9th ✰ Cathy says Pauline's left Kenny, gone to her mother's. I thought it was odd that I hadn't seen her. Lucy's off school with a cold so I haven't been out. I'd like to go and see her but I don't know where exactly her mother lives.

I picked up Cathy's list for the supermarket tonight. She looked so pretty and feminine and somehow vulnerable as she saw to the baby. All those little white things, tiny vests and bootees and the new bottles of lotion and talc in the little white basket lined with organza. She stayed in the hospital for five days in the end, her mother couldn't get down until the sixth and the hospital wouldn't release her to 'only a husband at home'. The baby, John Charles Brooks, was born on David's birthday, he was two weeks late and weighed 10 pounds 3 ounces only it was in grammes so Paul was two days working it out.

I've been thinking about Lilian's mother lately too. If I knew where she lived I'd go and see her.

Monday 20th ☆ Over a week since I last wrote. Don't know why.

Pauline came today, she looks terrible, weight has dropped off her, she was like chalk, huge bags under her eyes, chain smoking, sometimes not quite coherent, she must be on something for her nerves. Couldn't help but compare her appearance with Kenny's. He looks fine, saw him the other day. He said 'Pauline's left me and the kids.' Full of self-pity and with those childish petulant lips drooping.

Pauline is at her mother's but the children are still with Kenny. I was shocked to hear that, but I shouldn't have been, I should have known. She walked out, leaving Kenny to cope with the life she couldn't face, hoping that it would make him understand. She's out of her mind with worry about the children but at the same time thinks why *should* she be, they're with their father. At the moment she's in no fit state to cope with three children. I *wish* I could bring them here. Her hands shook all the time she was talking and she kept rubbing her face as if to de-fog her mind. She said within two days of her leaving Kenny had given up his job, was on Social Security and had a welfare officer calling. 'Wish I could have had that much help,' she said bitterly, 'perhaps things wouldn't have come to this.' She's asked Kenny to leave her alone to sort herself out but he won't. He telephones, he calls, he tries his little-boy-lost routine on her parents with good effect and Pauline is sickened. She's at loggerheads with her parents, doesn't see how she can stay there much longer. On top of all this, Pauline's younger sister has got herself pregnant. Pauline's mother said, 'We'll have to move, we'll have to move,' when she heard the news. Much the same reaction as when it happened to Pauline. 'What will the neighbours say?' The girl's seventeen and her parents say that she should marry the father of her baby. Pauline went berserk, told them they were Victorian and her sister that she was stupid.

David wants me to keep away, not to be involved.

Thursday 23rd ☆ David came home from work with a migraine this morning. He's been in bed all day. He's overtired, up at half-past six and not home till half-past six. This way of life's not good for either of us. All work and not enough pay for play.

It's the works do on the December 16th, I'll get to meet all those people who are only names to me now. The thought of it makes me feel nervous.

Saturday 25th ☆ D and I had all the kids' Christmas toys out tonight, playing with them and wrapping them. Bought some presents in Norwich today. Lucy and I went on the bus, racing round the shops in the dark rain, everywhere very festive and cheering. Treated ourselves to a large slice of coffee gateau. Lucy enjoyed it. She's full of Christmas and tries to explain all our family rituals to Katie. They're very precious to her, as they are to me. I'm constantly being brought up short by how like me she is. Bought some of D's favourite after-shave and an LP and yet more Christmas cards. Great to spend money without worrying.

Monday 27th ☆ We're ill, the children and me.

Dragged myself out of bed this morning and pulled some clothes on. My head was hot and aching, my limbs were stiff and difficult to move, knew I'd have to see the doctor. The children were the same, sore throats and burning. I dressed them as warmly as I could and fed them. Then, carrying Katie because she's in no fit state to walk and the pushchair's broken, poor Lucy had to walk, we staggered down to the village to telephone the doctor. The phone box was broken as usual. I groped my way across to Johnson's, poor little Lucy trotting behind in the foggy wet morning, and asked Peggy if I could use the phone. By the time I got through it was after ten o'clock so the doctor couldn't come to see me. The frosty receptionist left me in no doubt about that. I burst into tears right there in the stock room of the shop, Katie was so heavy, her head dropped on my neck, Lucy was so pale and tired. Peggy looked after us and asked John the butcher to run us home in the van. I was very grateful. But I'm not grateful to my every-loving husband. He is a hateful, unfeeling sod, wait till he has migraine again. He can't stand me to be ill. He was angry because there was no meal ready when he came home from work. After today and what I've struggled through, many would have given in, strong men would have cried. I languished with my children in an armchair by the fire.

He banged about the kitchen making himself an omelette and yelled ungraciously 'Do *you* want one?' I declined, preferring hunger. I don't like eggs and anyway broken eggs do not necessarily an omelette make, not when David's the cook. He made me a mug of tea, ' 'ere,' he said shoving a picture of the Queen crowned and smiling at her Jubilee under my nose. Wonder if she ever feels like this? Now that I have the 'flu, if that's what I've got, I know that I've never had the 'flu before.

Wednesday 29th ☆ I hate men. They're all idle pigs. He could have helped me over these last few days but he hasn't. He's been lost to us, wrapped up in the world of his current library book until I've broken into his thoughts and asked him to take Lucy and Kate up to bed. He thinks he's Mrs Britain because he's served up egg and chips twice. I couldn't eat it, so I did without food, which was the alternative. Lucy and Kate will eat anything that isn't green. Why *won't* he take over from me? I'm so *angry*. We haven't had a row, he knows naught of what boils inside my chest. I can't lash him with my tongue, it's pointless, because he genuinely doesn't understand, he really doesn't know what to do. I can't tell him every damned thing, every detail of housekeeping, I feel like a harridan as it is. Surely even a fool could see the toys need to be put away, the spills on the floor need wiping up. I wept today at the state of the house. Clothes scattered across the living room floor together with one toy money, two colouring books, assorted felt-tips and crayons, an eighteen-piece doll's tea-set, building blocks, a game with its contents all over the place and the torn pages of the *Radio Times*. The shade on the table lamp was tilted at a saucy angle, the potty, upturned, rested on the settee, a cup, a plate, an opened packet of biscuits and an overflowing ashtray decorated the coffee table which was covered with a fine layer of impacted crumbs and fingerprints. That was just the living room. Everywhere else was twice as bad. Would it have cost so much for him to have stayed home from work and take on my duties for one day? He doesn't care that his children have been neglected. No, that's not true, he doesn't *know* his children have been neglected. He would never think to bath them, to clean their teeth, to make sure they had something nourishing. I've never been too ill to cope before. It must have come as a shock to him. He'll have

to learn how to take over from me. I don't like all this resentment and anger building up inside me, it's unhealthy. And so is reasoning it away.

Thursday 30th ☆ Pauline's been. I was so embarrassed at the state of the place, she got stuck into the washing up and the tidying up, made me some coffee and sent all the kids upstairs to play. I was so ashamed, she told me not to be so stupid, I couldn't keep the place tidy when I was ill. But I kept thinking that she's see the inside of the cupboards or the cooker. My head is still ringing, I couldn't concentrate properly on what she had to say but she's back with Kenny. They've had a long talk and he's promised a fresh start. She thinks he only wants her back to keep house but things were impossible at her mother's and she's nowhere else to go. So it's hardly love's young dream. She didn't mention Jeannette so I didn't ask.

December

Friday 1st ☆ Nobody cares that I'm ill, except Leighton who said I look awful. David thinks I should be better by now. I said I probably would have been if I could have gone to bed. He says he's sorry, he hadn't realised how ill I was. I did tell him. I've tried to explain the difference between him doing as I ask with a resigned sigh and taking over my duties. He understands now, so he says. It's hell being indispensable.

Tuesday 5th ☆ It's bitterly cold. I froze waiting for Lucy to come out of school today. The house is still a tip, it's getting to me but the 'flu got there first. No one's coming for Christmas. My parents don't feel up to the trip, Simon and Sara won't come here for the same reason we won't go there, it doesn't seem fair to the kids. David's parents can't really come without his brothers who don't want to leave girlfriends and parties behind for a dull time here.

Cathy wishes she'd never bought the dining room suite. She daren't let the kids near it, she sits them on the worktops in the kitchen to eat but they keep sliding off. She says its murder they've nowhere to paint or play with plasticine and they've had to store the top of the old table under their bed, there is nowhere else.

Saturday 9th ☆ Annual pilgrimage to see Father Christmas in Norwich today. We stood for ages in the queue and tropical temperatures to see Santa Claus, frantically trying to keep Katie interested in black sheep baa-ing. Went to Jothan's as usual because they always have a good Father Christmas. I wouldn't want a Santa who shattered the children's innocent belief. My confidence tottered a bit today but all was well. Father Christmas wasn't on his throne when we got to the front of the queue, he was on the other throne, the one through the door behind the fairy and the sign marked Gents. He soon returned doing his flies up but, with great aplomb and sweeps of his cloak he hid it from the children – you wouldn't get that sort of quick thinking Santa at the Co-op. He told Lucy and Katie that he'd been up on the roof to make sure Rudolph was all right, any childish doubt firmly squashed. I went all weepy and emotional at the children's faces, always do. Spent Diana's ten pounds on them but it didn't go far. There were some magnificent toys and all at magnificent prices, and I thought we were rich. We will be rich one day, if I have to do a bank. I'll take Lucy and Kate to Harrod's and buy every tiny little thing that takes their fancy.

We lashed out on circus tickets today, it's David's new expansive mood. I nearly fainted at the cost of four ringside seats. We haven't told the children, it will be an after-Christmas surprise. They've never been before.

This was our last free Saturday before Christmas, felt quite sought after, 'Sorry, Paul Newman, I haven't a free Saturday left before Christmas.' It's the works do and the school fayre next week. David wants me to come to Norwich on my own one day next week to buy myself a new dress to wear. I looked in the shop windows today but didn't see anything that took my eye. I will have to have a new dress and Mrs J would probably have Katie for me so why am I reluctant? I don't really want to go, that's why. I don't know what the people will be like, there'll be no one I know. I'm an oyster that doesn't want to be prized out of its shell.

Sunday 10th ☆ I need loads of things for the works do, I'll have to get my hair done, don't know how to have it done. I haven't any make-up apart from what Sara's given me from time to time. It's all the wrong colours. I *do* want to look my best for David's sake. I'll *have* to have a dress. I expect Cath would lend me her fur jacket, probably an evening bag as well. David says I can spend what's left of the car money, he meant to be generous but I'm wondering if it will be enough. I'll need shoes too. Oh, I wish Diana was here, I don't know where to begin. All David has to do is bath and change.

Tuesday 12th ☆ Exciting parcels arrived from David's family today. The top of the wardrobe is looking healthier now, packages almost touching the ceiling.

I'm all sorted out now, Cathy's sorted me out. I'm going to Norwich on Friday, I'm to have my hair done at the place where Cath goes and she's told me how to have it done. I'm to buy a plainish dress to be on the safe side and it doesn't have to be long these days. I rather fancied floating around on marble balconies with yards of delicate silk. 'You're not going to Buckingham Palace, it's just the works do.' I have to go to Jothan's make-up counter where I'll find a girl wearing a golden brooch which says 'I'm Mandy'. She'll fix me up with what I need. I can borrow Cathy's jacket and bag, she and Pauline have thoroughly enjoyed themselves sorting me out. Pauline wishes she was going, I wish she was going too. I haven't been to anything like this for ages. I'm nervous. It's reading all those articles about impressing your husband's boss and my determination to be myself. I'll have to choose which it's going to be.

Friday 15th ☆ I'm not lovely. I don't suppose I ever was lovely, I just used to think I was. When I first realised, yesterday, that all the people at the works do aren't going to swoon with envy or lust at my gorgeous good looks, I was a bit sad. But today, in the hairdressers, when the realisation really went home, I was almost glad. It was relaxing. I'm not beautiful so that's that, I can quit all that *exhausting* effort, it's pointless when I know I can't achieve beauty. I'll just be neat and clean and presentable, it's so much easier.

Wandered round Norwich today. Felt strange to be on my own, first time it's happened. I felt I should have enjoyed it but I didn't. Was lost and lonely. I was uncomfortable in the hairdresser's. A very dishy, young man did mine. It was so hot and all those lights highlighting my skin defects in the mirror. I was the ugliest woman in the salon.

Dashed up to Cath's to show her what I'd bought and the hairdo when I got back. I didn't look so ugly then, the excitement had improved me and I look better on home ground then I do in flash stores. I bought a black dress, the skirt has millions of tiny pleats and a blouson effect bodice. I've got black patent high heels too, been practising walking in them, should be able to do it by tomorrow night. Hope my hair stays in. Mandy the make-up looked fed-up, chewed gum and didn't speak, she slapped the tubes of make-up into my palm and said 'Five fifty with the special offer' without closing her mouth. Frightened her lips would stick together I expect.

Mrs J says the kids were as good as gold. They enjoyed having them, wouldn't have worried if I'd known.

Saturday 16th ☆ It's been great, had a really good

157

time and sinful thoughts about Brad, David's boss. We were attracted to each other on first sight, sexy and thrilling to dance with him, knowing eyes and smiles behind our innocent conversation – lovely and lustful.

Hope the fights haven't put paid to any further 'do's'. I couldn't help but see the funny side of it. It was all down to Jock and his basic animal urges. I was a bit dubious when he asked me to dance, having seen Scottish 'hard men' on the telly, but he was the perfect gent, called me Mrs Bennett, felt like I should have enquired after the health of his family in true boss's wife tradition, but his wife and six children have left him, gone back to Glasgow. 'It's ma drinkin', d'ya see, Mrs Bennett?' He'd had too much then, before the meal, 'Ma drinkin' an' ma animal urges.' He was absolutely serious. A small thin man who'd done his best to look smart, but a tartan shirt, even with the black bootlace tie, just didn't come off with the crumpled light tan suit and the well-greased Tony Curtis haircut. His trousers hung baggy and creased round his suede shoes with the built-up crepe soles. I found out afterwards that apart from the shoes and tie they were the only clothes he has. 'Ah gave 'er money, ya know Mrs Bennett, she didna go short, an' ah never laid a hand on 'er, before God ah never laid a hand on 'er. But what could ah do Mrs Bennett, ah'm a man an' ya know men need ... but what am ah tellin' you fer, ah'm sure Mr Bennett ...'

'Oh yes,' I put in quickly, 'he ... erm ... he's a man.' I daren't laugh, he was from the Gorbals. I flashed a look across at David, he beamed like the Eddystone lighthouse. He was proud of me tonight, I could sense it and it felt great.

During the turkey dinner I saw Jock give a long slow meaningful wink to a large lady in apricot chiffon, someone else's wife. It was so unexpected it was comic.

Next thing, after the dancing had started again, the floor suddenly cleared and the music stopped, which was a mercy in itself. There was our amazon in apricot chiffon dragging Jock off her husband who was on the floor. David and Brad went to sort it out. I felt so proud of David tonight, he looked tall, dark, and handsome and every inch a gent. I can understand the problems he has at work after meeting everybody tonight. I do love him. I love David the man, it's David the husband I find hard to take.

The fight broke out again coming home on the hired bus. We were sitting behind Brad the Beautiful; some at the back were singing drunkenly, the husband of the snooty-looking girl from the office was horribly drunk. He sat facing into the aisle with one arm on the back of his own seat, the other on the back of the seat in front, staring at the floor, his eyes half closed, his face looked damp and highly coloured, his tie askew, tousled hair and his head jogging about with the movement of the bus. Every girl's dream looking like he was going to be sick. No wonder David made sure I sat by the window, it was for protection. Snooty Girl was looking firmly out of the window. Husband kept up an agonised wail to the floor, 'I'm sorry Gail. I'm sorry Gail.' It was a terrible thing to hear. Next thing Jock leaps to his feet shouting, 'An' so ah do. She *is* a fine lookin' woman. Ya want mi ta poot one on yer?' Everyone went quiet except the drunks at the back who went on singing, and dreamboat who kept on moaning, 'I'm sorry Gail, I'm sorry.' Some of the men pulled Jock back into his seat. 'Aw, come on Jock,' 'You've had too much. Sit down Jock.'

Brad leaned round the seat and said, 'I think we'll just give 'em all a turkey next year.' I was weak laughing. I'm so glad I went, don't know what I was afraid of.

159

Brad's wife didn't come, they'd had a row. I knew because when David said 'Shame Liz isn't here,' Brad carefully picked at the crumbs on the tablecloth and said 'yes, she couldn't make it.'

I feel more as if I belong in this area after tonight, being out with all those people and I certainly feel closer to David having seen who he works with, feel more a part of his life somehow. At the school fayre this afternoon the other mothers were friendly and all that but I felt out of place, a sense of not belonging. Even that feels better now. Thought of Lilian today, looking at the spread of home-made cakes and buns for sale, she would have been right in the thick of it, organising, her buns best of all. Leighton was Father Christmas, he's thinking of taking it up professionally, he likes the holidays. Pretty good for Leighton, expect he heard it somewhere.

Put the Christmas tree up today. I love to do that, I love Christmas and everything to do with it. Finished Lucy's costume for the school play tonight. It's a mad social whirl, we're going to Pauline's for supper on Tuesday, Cathy and Paul are going too. I think we're part of the new deal, we're the social life.

Tuesday 19th ☆ Pauline had gone to a lot of trouble for tonight's party. There were three different sorts of sandwiches, a blackcurrant cheesecake, because she knows I love it, bless her, nuts and crisps and sausages on sticks etc. I wanted to fling my arms round her when I saw it all. She's short of cash and far from happy but she's making such an effort. 'She's been slaving over a hot stove all day,' said Kenny nodding towards the sandwiches, 'and she took the chocolate yule log out of the box all by herself.' Everyone smiled and made jokey noises but he'd hit a sensitive spot, which is what he aims at. Pauline's face showed it.

160

The house is sinking under the decorations she's put up, miles of multi-coloured tinsel and a glittering emerald tree. We partied in the glow of the fairy lights and one table lamp so we couldn't see a lot. Felt that if I'd given Pauline thirty pence I'd have got to see Santa and been issued with a plastic toy. Glanced at Pauline. She was wrapped in thought, looking at David. Her eyes said it all. 'If only.' I felt really sorry for her. I don't know if it's David himself she really fancies or if it's just that he's everything she wants in a man. I looked at the three men standing together. Kenny didn't fare too well in the comparison ... a head shorter, no prospects, ambitions or intentions, trying to be liked, to be one of the boys and failing every time. He's so false. He's different towards us women, penetrating shafts of cynicism and bad temper to Pauline, a rather arrogant protector to Cathy and me, 'Are you all right down there, girls? Let me know if you want anything,' parting of the petulant lips, flash of the famous pearlies, charm oozing charm, we are ladies, Pauline isn't. We are ladies because we're married to David and Paul; if we weren't we'd be birds, pieces, bits of skirt.

Had a drink with Mrs J and Ernest when we got back. They're off to Geoff's tomorrow. They haven't asked me to look after the animals.

David turned up at the school play this afternoon. I was delighted to see him. He sat and watched while Pauline and I cried. Lucy was wonderful. Cathy couldn't come with both babies and had no one to leave them with as everyone was at the play. She was upset about that because Lyndsey and Gareth were in it.

Lilian's house is up for sale. Hugh and Edward have moved in with Hugh's mother and the older ones will go there in the holidays. Keep thinking of Lilian's mother.

Thursday 21st ✩ My Christmas spirit is fading already. Lucy broke up this afternoon, I broke up tonight. They've been howling round the house like festive banshees, Mary and Joseph en route for Bethlehem they said.

Mrs J and Ernest went off yesterday. They've left parcels for Lucy and Kate and their keys in case their pipes burst.

Cathy's two youngest ones have the flu. She's on her knees, up all night with one or the other and the new baby is on two-hourly feeds. Her mother's coming down tomorrow. Poor lass, I can almost see the manufacturers of Valium rubbing their hands.

Egg and chips for tea, traditional fare for the weeks before and after Christmas.

Christmas Eve is on a Sunday, which is nice. Means David and I may not have our traditional yuletide row. He comes from work every Christmas Eve thoroughly Brahms and Liszt and, as I'm usually up to my knees in mince pies and stone cold sober with the children round my feet, I'm never pleased when he passes out on the settee. Wonder what Brad the Beautiful is doing for Christmas?

Saturday 23rd ✩ All the Christmassy children's programmes on TV in the mornings. I long to watch, recapture forgotten feelings, but I can't, I've too many onions to pickle and puddings to boil. Don't know how I'm going to contain the children till Monday morning. They're over-excited. David says I've done it. I asked him to do the same for me but he hasn't – not yet – but there's time. Cleaned the house today and didn't get the ironing finished. Should have concentrated on the ironing and persuaded David to help with the cleaning. He can't iron, he told me so, he's sorry but there we are, he can't do everything.

Monday 25th ☆ He's been.

Thursday 28th ☆ After Christmas is awful, the anti-climax and the kids still claim they've nothing to play with. Haven't seen a soul and can't go visiting with everyone's husband at home.

We haven't got anything left to eat, the lettuce has gone off and what's left of the turkey smells foul, couldn't make a risotto with it even if I knew how. Hope we can find a shop open tomorrow, man cannot live on nuts alone.

Sunday 31st ☆ Stayed at home, nobody baby-sits on New Year's Eve, so David had to go up the Crown on his own, shame. Watched the usual fixed assortment of obscure Scottish personalities having a ball on the telly. It's hard to believe you're celebrating when you're TV-bound with your wine from the wood and Hamilton MacHamish your gay heeland host with a song on his lips and a skirt round his hips. How can anyone think it's remotely entertaining to sit at home and watch the rest of the world hooting and roaring? You have to be a sadist to work at the BBC on New Year's Eve. David came back after a dozen. He always says the place to be on New Year's Eve is at home with your family, that's what he always says. He flaked out on the settee and I woke him to toast in the New Year. We crept into the children's bedroom and kissed them goodnight.

Almost a year since I began this diary. Lucy will be six in a fortnight, starting her fourth term at school. I'll be thirty-one in March and David will be thirty-five in November. Katie will be three in April and by the end of this year she was house trained.

C'est la vie. I'd give up, but we're going to the circus tomorrow.